BRAD'S BOX

BRAD'S BOX

BY
MARY
ALEXANDER
WALKER

ATHENEUM **1988** NEW YORK

Atheneum
Macmillan Publishing Company
866 Third Avenue, New York, NY 10022
Collier Macmillan Canada, Inc.
First Edition
Printed in U.S.A.
10 9 8 7 6 5 4 3 2 1

LIBRARY OF CONGRESS CATALOGING-IN-PUBLICATION DATA
Walker, Mary Alexander. Brad's box.
Summary: The high school boy who arrives to spend a year as a boarder with fourteen-year-old Rose's Iowa farm family ultimately becomes part of that family, changing Rose's life and blooming into a maturity that wipes out his past.
[1. Farm life—Fiction. 2. Iowa—Fiction]
I. Title.
PZ7.W15362Br 1988   [Fic]   87-33658
ISBN 0-689-31426-4

For
Rochelle Langlois Walker
with love

BRAD'S BOX

Chapter 1

When the door opened, the black winter sky loomed outside, even though it was early evening and snow swirled in, glittering and sparkling as it caught the light. Brad set the big wooden box awkwardly at his feet. He looked at us in a bewildered way, rather like a cautious chipmunk who couldn't decide if we were friend or foe. We stared at him, then at the wooden box.

So this is Brad, I thought, my curiosity bubbling. Brad, who is coming to live on our farm with us—I mean, in *our* house.

His clothes looked brand new—not as if he had been wearing them on the Greyhound bus all the way from Alabama! They weren't even wrinkled!

Over his arm, a small blue nylon day pack swung, so new, the fold creases were still in it.

He was tall and skinny—almost bony—and his hair was shaggy, not long, just shaggy gold. He was pale, too, and the most striking thing about him was his eyes—deep brown. I take that back about the chipmunk. Baby-seal look, I thought, with those huge, intense brown eyes.

The poor guy was fidgeting. None of us had said a word. What a cold welcome for a stranger, I felt. Being the oldest, I should come up with something. I tried to drag my voice up from its hiding place, but it was Brad who spoke first.

"I—I—" he said, only when he said it, it didn't sound like "I" at all. "I know you from the snapshot, Rose. You look younger than fourteen," he said to me. Then, "Hello, Karen, Billy, and Sam."

His thick Alabama accent was too much—we laughed. My dad stamped in at that moment from putting away the car—snow scattering around him. He sputtered in exasperation at his ungracious children. Mother came in from the kitchen, dropping her role as an Iowa farm wife with her apron on the hall chair. Even though she had gone to nursing school in Indiana, she reverted to southern honeysuckle like a native plant returned to its own soil.

"Brad! How wonderful to hear that familiar southern accent. I miss it so, living among these clipped midwesterners." She extended her hand, only a little encrusted with biscuit dough, and said in a warm voice, "Welcome to our home—*your* home. We are so glad to have you here." She glanced at us with a bit of fire in her eye. "Aren't we?"

We were still standing stupidly, but we coughed, gulped, and gurgled various agreements in answer to

Mom's pointed question. She put her hand on Brad's sleeve, and leading him toward the roaring fire—all done up for the newcomer's benefit—she said, "Come by the fire. You must be frozen, unaccustomed as you are to this kind of winter. You can talk to the children later."

I watched them go into the living room, thinking how strange that nervous, tall figure looked in his— were they all new?—clothes, though they were regular-boy clothes, cords and a jacket. Somehow—

Billy and Sam interrupted my thoughts by dinking around with the big wooden box that Brad had set down on the floor when he came in. Drops of water stood on it where the snow had melted. It was old wood, and Billy rattled the padlock on the front.

"Hey, Brad," six-year-old Billy yelled. "Whatcha got in the box?"

"Yeah, what's in the box, Brad?" Sam is twelve.

Karen, eight, yelped, "I want to see in the box, Brad. Can we open it, please? Do you have the key?"

A shadow fell across us as they—well, we—all leaned down and tested the padlock to see if it was indeed locked. It was, and the shadow that had fallen over us was Brad, suddenly towering.

From the look on his thin, colorless face, we stepped back, stumbling almost, as he silently reached down, picked up the box, and hoisted it to his shoulder with the kind of grace that suggested it contained the crown jewels. He took a few steps and then stopped, as if he didn't know where he was going, and, of course, never having been in our house before, he didn't know. "If—if you'll say where, I'll take it to—to—to where I'm going to sleep," he stammered.

My dad had just finished changing his boots and said, "I'll show you, Brad."

We followed up the stairs as if Brad were the Pied Piper. Even Karen and Billy were almost quiet, whispering together, instead of shattering the atmosphere with their usual yells. Mother sleepwalked at the end of the line, lost in a dream of mild-wintered Alabama and homesick for her seven sisters, I suppose. She sometimes gets that look during the long Iowa snows.

We stopped at the door of Billy's old room, though Dad went in and Brad followed. Sam and Billy were sharing a room now at the end of the upstairs hall. Brad's eyes seemed to grow larger in his face—still holding the box, balancing it elegantly on his shoulder.

Dad said, "Just put it wherever you like, Brad. This is your room now."

Brad gingerly set the box on the floor. I was not moving until he opened it. I was dying to know what was in it, though it was probably just his collection of junk like everybody has.

Sam and Billy had edged into the room, and Sam said, "Well, aren't you going to open it? Does it have your clothes in it?" Sam suddenly became aware of something we hadn't seemed to notice. "Where's your suitcase, anyhow?"

Yes, I thought, where *is* your suitcase?

"Sam!" Mom's voice carried command. "That's

enough. Now, all of you go downstairs and let Brad have some privacy. He's had a very long ride on the bus."

She started shooing us away from the door, but she turned back to Brad and said, "Billy will come up and call you to dinner shortly."

Brad and Dad were talking in low tones as we left, and it didn't seem to be five seconds before Mom had quelled our questions with a look and we were in the kitchen doing our chores just as if it were any old ordinary night.

I changed my mind about "any old ordinary night" when I saw the supper we were going to have, though I didn't have *too* much time to inspect it because I was handed a mammoth stack of carrots to scrape. The smells were enticing enough—cinnamon with apples was an unmistakable scent permeating the steamy warm kitchen, and that was special! Scraping the carrots and watching the tiny orange strips make abstract designs in the bottom of the sink, I wondered about Brad. He didn't look too smart to me—bringing an old box he wouldn't even open. I'll bet he's a dropout, I thought. When Dad had told us that Brad was coming to live with us, he'd said that Brad was supposed to be very bright but was having a lot of trouble at home and at school. "Too many children and not enough money," Aunt Lily had written from Alabama. Aunt Lily is my mother's sister and knows everybody and everything in the small town where she lives. And she's always solving (she thinks) somebody's problems. Once she sent us five-year-old twin girls whose parents were severely injured in a car accident. We only had them for three months, but we all cried when they left.

Aunt Lily does her share, though. She was taking care of the *rest* of that large family while we had the little girls. She engineered this plan for Brad, of course. Dad was to help Brad finish high school, and Brad was to help Dad on the farm.

Well, five-year-old cute little girls for three months are fun, but a skinny high-school boy *for a year* is something else again.

I had serious doubts about the whole thing from the first. The trouble is that my parents are not really democratic—not with us kids, anyway. They make the decisions and expect us to abide by them. When they told us about Brad's coming to live with us, I asked if he was supposed to be a hired man.

"No."

"A boarder, then?"

I knew about boarders because a lot of high-school kids from distant farms board during the week with families who live closer to school. My Aunt Bessie has a deliciously hunky basketball player, Brent Wilkinson, boarding with her.

"No, not a boarder. He's to be more like family, treated like family by all of us."

They didn't even ask my opinion; they just told us a little about Brad and said it was something they both wanted to do. I told them what I really wanted was a new dishwasher, I mean besides Sam and me, a mechanical dishwasher to replace our broken one, instead of another added plate and glass and silverware to wash. They both looked at me and said nothing. End of discussion.

"Rose, at the rate you are going"—my mother's voice sliced into my thoughts—"we won't have supper before next Sunday!"

"Oh, I thought this *was* Sunday, the way you're cooking up a storm," but I grinned when I said it. When my mother puts her head to it, we are all proud to have a guest at our table. Even if it is farm cooking, she's a master at it.

She was leaning down, checking something in the oven, when she answered, "I know, Rose, but—well," and suddenly she turned around and gave me the full blaze of her gray eyes, her voice soft. "If *you* ever had to go away to live with another family, I would hope with all my heart they would make you welcome." Her eyes filled, and she grabbed me and hugged me close for an instant. It startled me and touched me as well, and for the first time, I tried to imagine what it must be like—to be catapulted into a new family, like being snowbound in a completely new place, away from everyone you have ever known.

I think I grew just a fraction in that instant, and I also remembered why it is I usually forgive my parents for their authoritarianism.

It's harder, though, to forgive them for having farming for a livelihood: There's so much *work*! Animals to feed, feed to grow, planting, nurturing, harvesting, freezing, canning, and we never have a summer vacation.

I wasn't being really fair, though. We have a wonderful winter vacation before Christmas when we all go to Des Moines for the weekend. Dad takes Sam and Billy wherever they want to go, usually a college basketball tournament. Mother and Karen and I go shopping and lunch at some elegant place. And this year we all went to the Ice Follies. I gazed toward the dark window, but I really was seeing that beautiful skater in the feathery silver costume, gliding under the spotlight, the sparkles in her hair. . . .

"Rose!"

Mother's voice toppled me from my reverie, and I turned back to the carrots with more enthusiasm, then tossed them with the walnuts and seasoning my mother had left on the cutting board.

By that time, I wasn't surprised that Mom had set out Great-Grandmother's cut-crystal bowl for the salad. I was proud of the way it looked with the carrot strips and walnuts.

When I carried the bowl into the dining room, Karen and Billy were just finishing setting the table and having an argument about who would sit by Brad. Already he has admirers, I thought, though I'm not one of them. Then, remembering my mother's words, I revised my thoughts to consider that I might at least *try* to like him. Billy caught my attention by pulling Karen's hair. She burst into tears, striking out at him in a fury with her little fists.

"Whoa, there, you two," I said, pulling them apart and putting an arm around each but being sure they couldn't reach each other.

"What's going on in there?" called Mom.

"Nothing, Mom," I answered. "It's okay."

Then I whispered to them, "Cut it out. Do you think Brad is going to want to sit by either one of you if you act like that?" I dried Karen's tears and she started in, "But I want—"

"Okay, look. Just for tonight—if it's okay with Dad, you can sit on this side of Brad, Karen—"

Billy immediately started to yell. "She always gets her way—"

"And, Billy," I said quickly, "you can sit on the other side of Brad. Okay?"

They eyed each other for a moment, and I continued to stand between them.

"You've done a lovely job on the table, kids." And they had. The bright green checked cloth was family fare, but it was starched crisp, and the white napkins were stiff and snowy. A low bowl of winterberries, bright orange, glistened in the center of the table.

My mother came in, carrying a steaming casserole of creamy potatoes au gratin, the melted cheese still bubbling on the top.

"Oh, the table looks lovely, Billy, Karen. And the salad, Rose." She inspected everything with a sweep of her eyes. "Billy, go up and get your father and Brad. Sam should be in any moment with more wood for the fireplace."

I helped Mom bring the last things in to the table, and by that time, everyone was seated except the two of us. The pork chops, double and stuffed with sage dressing, and the homemade biscuits made the whole room smell delicious. While my dad said grace, as we always do in my family, I thought I would die from an overdose of wonderful smells. It *was* a beautiful supper—and I glanced at Brad to see if he appreciated it. His brown eyes fairly glowed. Yes, he was going to enjoy my mother's cooking.

As soon as we all had a plate of food in front of us and Brad had complimented my mother on how good everything tasted, Billy attacked the subject of Brad's box again. Sometimes he's a real pest, but I was glad he was asking all the questions I wanted answers to and knew better than to ask. "If Brad doesn't let me see what's in the box, I'm going to take my hammer and *wham! wham!*—I'll break it open and I'll get to see what's in it! Ha!" His eyes sparkled with mischief. "And I'll show you, too, Sam."

My mother gasped. Dad almost choked on the pork chop he was chewing.

Before they could intervene, Brad's gawky, shy, baby-seal look disappeared. I found myself staring at a young man with a determined jaw, head held up, and his eyes like fathomless brown caves with a fire burning deep inside.

"That box is very valuable to me," he said, looking at each of us in turn and then focusing firmly on Billy, "and none of you are to try to open it—ever."

Chapter
2

W e couldn't have been much more astonished if he had said it contained a time
bomb. I couldn't care less about his childish little se-
crets, but I did admire the way he'd handled that tiger-
ish Billy. Dad didn't say a word, but I thought I saw a
little smile twitch at the corner of his mouth, as if the
matter had been settled without his help—and that he
was amused that Billy had met his match.

Mom changed the subject by asking Brad if he
knew her other sisters besides Aunt Lily. All the rest of
them have the names of flowers, too, and I am named
for the youngest, Rose. If those southerners must use
flora for their names, I have always been secretly grateful Mom didn't name me after Aunt Amaryllis. Brad
said the only one he knew was Aunt Iris because she
works in the local grocery store.

My mind drifted away from them to my own life
and school the next day, wondering if my green sweater
was clean enough to wear and wondering if I might

possibly have a reason to drop by my Aunt Bessie's, my father's sister, after school, as she has that boarder, Brent Wilkinson. I was dreamily chewing a walnut and thinking, Brent Wilkinson. Even his name is beautiful. . . .

"Rose—Rose! Will you help clear the table while I get the dessert?"

I jumped, swallowing my walnut, and stood up. Brad stood up, too, and without another word, he picked up plates on the other side of the table and carried them into the kitchen, just like family. But he is family, I said to myself—well, kind of.

Mom brought in the dessert, and Sam, because it's his favorite, shimmered like neon. "Spicy apple crunch pie! Oh, Brad, go away tomorrow and come back tomorrow night so we can welcome you again!"

That got a laugh from everyone, and I could agree with him, as the aroma of cinnamon and apples from the still-warm pie drifted around the table. A pitcher of heavy cream was passed around for the pie and I felt I couldn't move, much less wash dishes.

But wash dishes I must, though Sam and I take turns and Karen and Billy have cleanup jobs, too. Brad came in the kitchen to help us, though I heard Sam whisper to him as I plunged my hands into the hot, soapy water that he should take it easy while he could. Brad stayed, anyway, and Sam quizzed him about the basketball team at his former high school.

Basketball reminded me of the next day, and what it might bring. How were my friends going to receive this new—new what? I settled for "newcomer" and stole a glance at him as he talked to Sam. He certainly didn't score many points for looks: skinny, pale. Not that he was ugly, exactly, and his hair wasn't a bad color, kind of brown-gold, but the cut, or rather the uncut shag. . . . But I did have to give him points for his eyes. They were incredibly beautiful; not a weak chin, no, a strong jaw. Okay, another point. Mouth? Nice-shaped lips, but somehow tight, nervous, so that he didn't have a cheerful look. Tall. I sighed. I didn't think he would be an asset to my social life where my girlfriends were concerned. As for the rest of the school, I was only a sophomore and didn't have any status of my own. I surely couldn't afford to carry him. I wondered if my parents had thought about that. That he just might be an embarrassment to me at school—and that accent! I almost groaned. Maybe I did groan, because Brad suddenly said, "What's the matter?" though he says it "maddah."

Poor guy—he only illustrated the very point I had been making to myself.

"Oh, nothing. Just thinking there seem to be a lot of dishes," I answered.

"Rose, only one more plate than usual!" said Sam. "That's not very nice of you."

I blushed. "Oh, I didn't mean *that*—"

When I finished the dishes I was bone-tired. I had been worrying about Brad's arrival without knowing it until he appeared. Now I was going to be tense about how he would be received. I dried my hands and went to get my homework.

I made a resolution: Brad is not going to be my problem. My parents took this on and they can just worry about it themselves. Family! He's not *my* family.

I opened my math book on the floor by the fire, but the numbers blurred before my eyes. I hope he is not going to be in my classes, and I hope I don't have to take him anywhere. I am going to spend as much time as possible at Aunt Bessie's. Brent Wilkinson. What a lovely name.

A heavenly thought crossed my mind: Why couldn't Brent live with us instead of Brad?

Chapter
3

_F_ ortunately, my parents didn't ask me to go with Brad to register at school the next day; I already had a plan in case they did. I was leaving early to go by Laurie's house to check my math before school. As it was, I missed a ride because Dad took the morning off from farm chores and drove Brad to school himself because it was Brad's first day.

It was a long, cold walk to reach Laurie's, bright and beautiful after the snowfall last night. The crisp air stung my nose as I walked through that white fairyland, the sun hitting the brilliant mounds and hills and the newness of the snow sparkling in pristine purity. The powder silenced my footsteps. I became a graceful dancer, kicking the glittering snow dust into the air, watching the sun strike the bits and turn them for an instant into tiny rainbows—reds, blues, and golds before they vanished magically. I couldn't help but wonder what Brad would think of this morning wonderland, coming from the warm, still-flowering South as he did.

Maybe he won't even like it, I thought, remembering the snapshots Aunt Iris had sent us of her pale pink camellias blooming at Christmastime.

I looked up when I heard a shout. It was Laurie waving frantically, and I ran toward her.

"Rose, you are dawdling, for Pete's sake!" She was breathing rapidly, and a cloud of white smoke almost enveloped her red face—the warmth of her breath misting quickly.

"You are going to make us both late!"

She marched ahead, snow flying around her tiny feet.

Laurie is petite, small hands, small feet, and her body goes straight up and down, much to her despair. Her bosom, waist, and hips measure almost exactly the same. Aunt Bessie tells her that in her day there was the famous model, Twiggy, who was like that, but Laurie cannot be consoled.

But Laurie is pretty, really pretty. Her hair is in short, bronze curls all over her head, with matching long—and I mean long—bronze eyelashes. Her eyes are crystal-clear blue, and she has just a few light golden freckles on her nose like a dusting of pollen. Just then, she was frowning over her shoulder at me, looking up because I'm taller and urging me to hurry.

"Don't slow down," she said, "but I want to hear all about Brad—come on, what's he like?"

I was already panting to keep up with her, and the cold air hurt my chest. Before I could answer, she continued.

"Well, is he a hunk? Is he exciting? Is he nice? Do you like him? How did the family—"

"Good grief, Laurie, give me a chance!" I said, laughing. "No, he's not a hunk. No, he is not exciting. Yes, he is nice—well, kind of. I don't know whether I like him yet. The family was real nice—Billy and Karen were fighting over him. . . ." My breath ran out, what with keeping up with Laurie and the cold air bursting my lungs. "And he's kind of secretive," I gasped.

"What do you mean, secretive? How could he be secretive already? He's only been in your house"—she started figuring the hours and gave it up—"just a few hours. He hasn't had time to tell you his whole life story!"

"Oh, cut it out, Laurie. Do you want to hear this or not?" I asked, irritated.

"I'm sorry, Rose. I do want to hear it," she answered.

"Okay, Laurie, but you have to promise not to tell. The folks gave us a long lecture on letting Brad make his own way without—well, without our talking about his background or troubles or anything."

Laurie looked at me in a bewildered way.

"What I mean," I explained, "is that the people here, at school and everything, should make up their own minds without our saying anything about his having trouble at school or his family having money trouble or anything. You see?"

Laurie shook her head understandingly.

"So you have to promise, Laurie."

Laurie rolled her eyes to heaven and sighed. "I promise, Rose, I promise!"

"Okay," I whispered. "Brad brought this huge wooden box, and it has a padlock on it—and that's all he brought! Just a tiny day pack, no suitcase, no nothing. That's all!"

"Oh, it probably has his clothes in it, Rose." Laurie walked on as if she had lost interest, but I caught her arm.

"No, I don't think so. All his clothes, I mean the ones he was wearing, looked brand new—as if he hadn't ridden the Greyhound bus from Alabama in them for days!"

Laurie began to look interested.

I blabbed on, "And he won't let anybody look in the box—and he told us all to stay away from it. He said it was very valuable to him—he said it in front of the whole family!"

"You're kidding. Did he really? Then it doesn't sound like it holds clothes—you're right." Laurie's brow was wrinkled. "Do you think maybe your father bought him some new clothes before he arrived? No, *after* he arrived, when he got off the bus, maybe? What time was it?"

"He went to pick him up in town about four—the stores would have still been open. You know, Laurie, I think that explains it."

"Maybe he was in rags, Rose, his knees sticking out in the cold, his feet bare—" Laurie has a vivid imagination. I laughed.

"Oh, Laurie! Maybe his clothes were just too light for this climate. Don't get carried away—and don't tell anybody!"

"Don't say that again, Rose. I am a trustworthy person," she said firmly, sticking her snubby nose in the air. It was too short to rise very far, but it gave the right effect, anyway. She *is* a trustworthy person, too.

Laurie stopped. "Okay, I can see the school. We can slow down a bit."

"Thanks a lot," I breathed.

We could see other students now, their bright jackets and hats standing out against the snow like bits of colored candy.

"I love it when it looks like this, don't you, Laurie?"

Laurie wrinkled her nose at me in a grimace, her blue eyes reproachful under her striped woolly cap. "Don't try to change the subject, Rose. Doesn't he have any redeeming qualities, or is he just going to be a burden and a bore, a sack of rocks around your neck?"

I winced inwardly. Laurie was only repeating the words I had said to her last week when I was telling her my fears about Brad's arrival.

"Well," I said, shifting my books, since my fingers were beginning to feel as brittle as icicles, "I give him a couple of points for having beautiful eyes, and he's tall, and—and he doesn't have a weak face, though it's a kind of nervous face—uh—tight around the mouth—"

"I'm not surprised if the guy is nervous—imagine, Rose, if you suddenly had to move in with a family who weren't even *relatives* and start going to a new school and everything." She stopped, a small plume of snow glittering around her feet. "Gee, now that I think of it, I can't even think of any of my *relatives* I would want to move in with." She gave me a somber look, as if I didn't already feel guilty.

"Of course, Laurie. Believe me, you would have thought the family was entertaining Prince Charles— no kidding," I said hastily. "My mother put on a spread that would have tempted anybody." I told her about the supper and the extra-big roaring fire—Laurie loves my mom's spicy apple crunch pie, and she was looking wistful before I finished.

"Gee, I'm sorry you didn't ask me over. Think your family might take in another waif—a poor girl whose mother likes to feed her stew?"

I laughed. "You know we have our share of stew, Laurie!"

We waved at the Teague twins as we neared the door to the school, and Laurie smiled. "Yeah, but *your* mother's stew is good!"

Terri Teague giggled all the way to us and then pulled us together conspiratorially.

"I'll bet if you had known Brent Wilkinson and Pogey Holland were walking behind you, you would have slowed down!"

I turned around to look just as Brent and Pogey were almost behind us.

"Uh—hello, Brent." His royal blue parka matched his royal blue eyes. I was so dazzled I couldn't think of anything else to say. Then I remembered I hadn't spoken to Pogey, though he wouldn't care, anyway. "Hi, Pogey," but I hated to drag my eyes away from Brent.

"Hello, Laurie. Hi," Brent said to me, without really slowing down.

"Uh—uh—is my aunt's cold better, Brent?" I was struggling to slow him down any way I could. It worked—he turned around with a puzzled look. "A cold? Well, she was up making blueberry pancakes early this morning. She's okay."

Pogey groaned. "Blueberry pancakes. And I had wheat hearts, yuk," and they walked away laughing.

Laurie and the twins were waiting for my reaction, and I couldn't disappoint them. I screwed my face into an exaggerated worried pout and said, "My Aunt Bessie sounds really bad off. Don't you think I should go over there and check on her, be sure she's all right?"

They doubled over with laughter as we entered the building. Through the dark hall, silhouetted against the light, I saw a specter approaching. My heart sank. I knew it was Brad—he was going to be in my Lit class. So much for luck, bad luck.

Chapter 4

*T*he Lit class was above my level. I had only been allowed to take it because I had had all *A*'s in composition and the surveys. I had been so proud and I loved that class—until now. I suddenly wished I was with Laurie and my cronies in their regular old, plodding, dull class with Mr. Marfy, the regular old, plodding, dull teacher. Oh, how I wished it.

Brent Wilkinson was in this class, too—but only because he failed it and had to take it again. He didn't fail because he's dumb, but because basketball practice took up so much of his time. I liked the teacher, too, a frail, white-haired little bundle of fossil bones known as Miss Dallaway. She was tough, but she loved her material and must know everything there is to know about literature. Oh, Brad, I thought, why couldn't you just take something else—band instruments or something? They teach band in the field house way out by the football stadium, about as far from this class and me as one could get.

"Hello, Rose." Brad stopped beside me at the door, but I kept going, smiling just enough to say, "Hi," and hastened to my assigned seat. Thank goodness I was in the middle of the room, surrounded by other students, with no empty seats nearby. I opened my book and stuck my nose in it, but I knew that Brad was handing Miss Dallaway an entrance slip. I could hear her murmuring to him over the bustle of the students entering the class.

Finally, when it was quiet, she introduced him to the class, and he blushed when everyone turned around and looked to the back of the room where he was seated.

That wasn't the worst, though. When Miss Dallaway had the class started and was lecturing, she suddenly asked Brad if this was the area in literature he was studying—and he answered. It was the first time the class had heard his accent, and they roared. He brought down the house. I was embarrassed for myself—soon everyone would know he was living at our house—but my heart also went out to him. I sneaked a look with my lowered head, and to my shock and surprise, Brad was laughing, too. He was just laughing away as if he didn't care! Furthermore, he looked good when he laughed. Well, I thought, I've got a lot to learn about this guy. He's stranger than I thought. Then I had a little nudge from my brain—maybe *he's* laughing because *we* sound funny to *him*? Is this possible? I will have to get Laurie's analysis of this situation. Anyway, I lucked out the rest of the day—that class was the only one we had together. I could breathe more easily as I walked home that evening with Laurie. She was convinced that we probably *did* sound funny to him, but that his manners were too good for him to make a big thing out of it. *Hmmm.*

At supper that night—we were back to our usual style and had beef vegetable soup, corn bread, and lemon squares—Dad asked Brad how things had gone, and all he said was, "Fine." He took a stack of books up to his room after he helped with the dishes.

Laurie was right, now that I noticed. He does have good manners. Courtesy, my mother says, is the art of making other people feel comfortable. Perhaps he did have some of that, but he certainly made me uncomfortable, just by being around at school. Or was I making myself uncomfortable?

He didn't make Sam uncomfortable. Sam took to going into Brad's room after supper, though Mother insisted we could only go in when asked. I don't know if he asked Sam in or not, but he didn't throw him out. Sam began to act as if he had acquired a big brother and actually began to strut around the junior high school. He had this notion of "we men" or some macho foolishness like that. Billy and Karen had to go to bed earlier, or they would have been falling all over him, too, probably. I noticed that nobody seemed to have found out what was in the box, though, and one night washing dishes, I asked Sam about it.

"Since you and Alabama are so friendly, did he tell you what he's got in the box?"

"No, but he's a good guy and I bet he'll show me sometime."

"When will that be?" I asked, grinning with malice, secretly hoping he would show Sam so Sam could tell me. I had told the Teague twins about the box because it was such a good story, and now they were dying to know what was in it. Laurie would never have told it; she was miffed and told me I was untrustworthy. Sometimes she's such a Sunday school teacher—actually, she *is* a Sunday school teacher at the Community Church—but I said it was *my* secret to tell if I wanted to. It wasn't *her* secret. And, also, I wanted to know what was in it for myself, but I wouldn't tell that.

I wouldn't let Sam off the hook. "Come on, Sam. When is he going to show you what's in the box?"

Sam stalked off, muttering, "Aw, be quiet. Girls don't understand nothing."

Chapter 5

*B*rad and I didn't have much to say to each other. Though he should have been farther ahead, according to his age, he had lost a semester somewhere. He had a heavy schedule and was even doing an independent study with one of the history teachers. His nose was usually in his books, upstairs or downstairs, but at least twice I thought I heard him going downstairs quietly late at night. Straining my ears, I thought I heard the back door click: Wow, what would my father say about *that*? Plenty, I'll bet, though it didn't seem to matter to either Mother or Dad that he might be an embarrassment to me at school or that he was downright mean about not telling me what was in the box.

I just ignored him as much as possible. He didn't say anything at all in class unless he was asked. When he started talking, everybody still laughed. By the time Miss Dallaway got them stopped, it turned out usually that he was just trying to say, "I don't know. I haven't caught up yet." He wore a kind of cautious look a lot of the time, as if he were wary of what might happen to him next.

One afternoon, Laurie and I were walking behind Brad, going home from school. We hunched to the bitter wind, crunching the icy snow under our feet. Brad mostly walked alone, but this bleak day he was with three other boys. I could hear Pogey Holland. Pogey was laughing, but he wasn't being friendly.

"Say, Alabama, how do you manage to get all that southern molasses in your talk? Ah declare, it do make me think of corn pone and grits, sho' nuff."

To my surprise, Brad just grinned and kept on walking. The other boys were laughing, too. Pogey started in again.

"And Ah do hear other things about you all, too. Ah do hear you all have a box of very special things that you all keep padlocked. Did you hear that, men? Padlocked! Now, what's in that box, Alabama? Your little bitty, teensy-weensy baby shoes, maybe?"

That really cracked the boys up. They fell all over each other laughing, but my eyes were on Brad's face. He stopped. His arm shot out, grabbing Pogey by the collar of his shirt, pulling him forward. Brad's eye glittered and his voice was firm and low. He was no taller than Pogey, but he seemed to grow right there.

"You wouldn't understand, boy, anything of such importance, so mind your own business," he growled. When he let go of Pogey's collar, Pogey seemed to sag, his eyes still wide with amazement. Brad walked on

— 30 —

with the same unhurried step, while the three of them stood looking after him. Laurie and I fairly crept by, but they had nothing to say to us.

That night at dinner, Billy said, "Say, Dad, I heard Brad had a fight after school today with Pogey Holland. Old Pogey made some crack about Brad's box and Brad let him have it, right in the nose. Then he grabbed him like this and"—Billy jumped up from the table— "and with a left to the jaw and a right," he demonstrated a ferocious battle while my father motioned him to sit down. Billy sat down, enormously pleased with himself.

"There wasn't any fight, Dad," I said. "I was an eyewitness, and not a blow was struck by anyone. Billy is exaggerating."

Dad looked at me slowly. "I wonder how Pogey knew about Brad's box."

My heart sank. The Teague twins, of course; and everyone at the table would know who'd told them. Billy, Sam, and Karen were still in lower school. I wanted to look at my plate because I could feel my face turning pink. Brad's "manly" voice—I mean his deep one—broke the silence.

"Oh, I don't think anyone told Pogey about it, Mr. Carthage. I believe we saw those boys the night I came in. You remember there were some fellows hanging around the bus station when you came to meet me?"

"Yes," Dad said slowly, "that's true. I should certainly hope that the private affairs of this household would not be published by any of the members of it."

I felt my father's eyes on me, but I wasn't going to

take the chance of finding out. I was eating as if a ban was declared on food, effective in the next three minutes.

I was helping finish the dishes—it was Sam's night to wash—when Brad dumped his stack of books on the big, round oak kitchen table. As I started to leave the room, I wanted to speak to him, but I hardly could get up the courage.

All ready to bolt through the door, I said, "Thank you, Brad, for getting me out of trouble."

"Just a minute, young lady," he said.

I stopped.

"If you don't want me to embarrass you further—I mean, if it hurts you to have a poor, dumb cluck living here—"

"Oh, Brad, I don't think *that*—I—" I stammered.

He grinned and shoved his Lit book across the table. "Well, I can get a lot smarter faster if you'll just help me catch up on some of this and you won't have to be ashamed of me."

I knew I was blushing furiously, but I sat down; Brad and I began our first of many study sessions. In a month, *he* was helping *me*. That hurt my pride somewhat, but he consoled me by saying that it wasn't his brain that was better, but the value of his "age and experience" at seventeen. After all, he was *supposed* to be ahead of me.

The other students seemed to have forgotten about his accent; at least they stopped laughing, and they stopped asking about the box. Inside the family, our curiosity still burned. Billy frankly nagged Brad to open the box. Sam had been caught trying to work the lock. Coward that I am, I just kept hoping that Brad would sometime like us well enough to open the box and show us what was in it.

One day, when Brad was helping Dad get the tractors ready for spring plowing, Sam signaled to me from the door of my room. I followed him to Brad's door. He motioned me to the box.

"Look," he said, "there's dust all over the top except where he's got his stuff stacked—even on the lock."

"So?" I asked, wanting to know desperately, but afraid of venturing too far into Brad's den.

"Well, that means he doesn't have anything in it that he uses. Let's see how heavy it is."

I couldn't resist it. Hypnotized with curiosity, I carefully stacked the books on the floor.

Sam put his hands under one side and I put mine under the other. We lifted it easily.

"Not too heavy, whatever he has in it," said Sam.

"Rock it. Let's see if it rattles," I said, lifting my end.

"Not a sound. Must have it packed in tissue paper."

"Tip it slowly and see if you hear anything slide, Sam," I said, straining to hear so much as a rustle in the box.

The rustle I heard came from behind me. My mother was standing in the door, wearing a Queen Victoria face. We almost dropped the box, but gently we

— 33 —

set it down, fearfully replacing the books and pencils—even in their same places so the dust was not disturbed.

"You have violated the privacy of an invited guest in this house."

Sam and I followed her out as if she were leading us by a string. You couldn't have paid me to go into Brad's room after that. My mother's anger cut my sleuthing to nothing . . . for a while.

Chapter
6

S leuthing. One thing I wanted to know _for sure_ was if Brad really was sneaking out at night. If those really were his footsteps I heard—or was I dreaming—going ever so lightly down the stairs. Could it be Sam? No, I didn't think so. And where could anybody _go_? Way out in the country the way we were and so cold it made me shiver just thinking about it. And I never heard anyone come back, but then I'm not too good at staying awake. I wondered if maybe I should ask Sam about it. I thought it was rather sneaky of Brad, after my dad had been so nice to him, but I was going to be _sure_ before I said anything to Dad or to Brad.

Two weeks later, during one of our study sessions, I rose from my chair to make chocolate, and Brad, knowing my intentions, got up, too; he reached for the cocoa and sugar while I scrabbled under the cabinet for a pan. I poured out the milk and was waiting for it to heat while Brad finished the last paragraph on his English paper.

Somehow my mind drifted to the girls in the senior class, and I thought of the Senior Sweetheart Dance coming up. Brad hadn't said anything about going, so I thought he had decided against it. I was curious as usual, though, and the question popped out. "If you were going to the Senior Sweetheart Dance, who would you ask?"

If I thought he would hem and haw around, I couldn't have been more wrong. He wrote his last word and then looked up. Without hesitating for a moment, he said, "Meridal Larson." Then he returned to his paper, holding it up to read for his revisions.

Meridal Larson! I was surprised. Meridal is really ordinary looking—I mean, she has nice brown hair and slanty brown eyes, and she isn't ugly or anything like that, but she's not really slender like the models on TV. Her body is—well, her body is just a body with all its parts in the right places, but nothing special. I could see her clearly in my mind's eye—just plain old Meridal in the blue corduroy slacks and plaid shirts she wears all winter, just like the rest of us. She has a nice smile, though, and she uses it a lot. But, still, considering the standouts, the knockouts, among the senior girls, I was surprised. And I did a really thoughtless, mean thing at dinner the next night.

The family had just said grace, and Dad was asking Brad how things were going at school. Before Brad could answer, I piped up, "He would like to ask Meridal to the Senior Sweetheart Dance."

Brad looked at me as if I had broken a trust, and when his face grew crimson with embarrassment, I wished my devilish tongue would stick forever to the roof of my mouth.

Billy screeched, "Brad's got a girlfriend, Brad's got a girlfriend!"

Dad gave Billy such a laser-beam look that he hushed, but Karen's face screwed up as if she were going to cry. By then, she believed with all her heart that Brad was going to marry her when she grew up. She idolized him. It was disgusting the way she tried to follow him everywhere.

Mother gave me a stare that simply defied description because it was half and half: half hurt that I had so completely forgotten my sense of courtesy—and half angry. I was in for it now. I dared not meet Dad's eye. I stared into my stew as if searching for something. My ears were burning.

Somewhere out of this chaos, I heard Brad's voice. He, at least, had gained control, and horror of horrors, he was speaking my name.

"Rose?" His voice was deep.

Slowly I raised my eyes as dead silence fell around the table. His dark eyes were staring a hole through me, his face solemn.

"Rose, you misunderstood me. Meridal is not my girl, nor do I want her to be." He paused, and I wanted desperately to pull my eyes away but I felt hypnotized.

He continued after a moment. "The reason I would have asked her to the dance is that I think she is a comfortable girl to be with, to talk to—and I haven't found that to be true with the others."

Nobody at the table made a sound. Why didn't Billy knock over his glass of milk or Karen drop her fork or something like they do every meal? No, everybody had to witness this humiliating scene.

Brad's eyes never left my face for an instant. "Also, Rose," he said slowly, "Meridal was the only person in the senior class who went out of her way to make me welcome at school, to show me around, to speak to me whenever she saw me, no matter who she was with."

I was feeling worse and worse. I wondered if I wasn't going to be sick. Oh, I wished I knew how to just turn pale and faint—faint dead away on the floor. Would he never stop, and wouldn't the family stop acting as if the curtain had just gone up at a play? Traitors, all of them.

But had Brad finished? Oh, no, I had to be held over the grill some more.

"So you see, Rose, the feeling I have for Meridal is that of a friend, but I would tell anyone, anyone at all, that I admire the person she is—basically kind. Don't you think so, Rose?" he asked.

I swallowed, temporarily unable to speak, but as he waited, his face questioning, I found my voice and croaked, "Yes, I do think so," hoping that now dinner would resume. But I deserved it all, I knew I did, and worse. I shoved a fork into my stew. Since I was going to hate myself forever for being such a bigmouth, I might as well eat, even if it tasted like straw.

"And, Rose?" Brad's voice again.

I could not raise my eyes.

"Rose?" he said again.

My mother nudged me with her foot under the table, just as Billy shrieked with glee. "Rose, Brad's talking to you!"

"Thank you, Billy. I haven't lost my hearing," I said, glaring at him.

I sighed and looked resignedly at Brad. A small smile was playing at the corners of his mouth. "Since you seem to have an interest in my attending the Sweetheart Dance—not that I can dance—why don't you come with me? That handsome basketball player— what's his name?—anyway, perhaps you can renew your acquaintance with him."

Billy was immediately in the middle of it. "Whoops! Rose is going to get a basketball play—" but Mother had quelled him before he could finish.

If looks could kill, Brad would have flopped over lifeless on the dining-room floor. I was so angry that I would have brought up—*right then*—about sneaking out at night. If I had only been sure. I would have aired it in front of everybody since he'd dared to bring up Brent. As it was, I wanted to bite off a corner of the oak table and spit it across the room at him!

"Brad, how could . . ." I began, stammering with fury.

"Well," he interrupted, "how about it? Will you go?"

Mother joined in, maliciously. "Of course she will, Brad. She's a kind person, too." She turned to me: "Aren't you a kind person, dear?"

Trapped. Trapped.

Sam, my own brother, who had been quiet the whole time, said sarcastically, "Yeah, Mom, she's one of the kindest people I know."

"Not 'yeah,' Sam," Mother corrected, and then, smiling too brightly, "I'm sure Bessie can make you a lovely new dress. She's been just waiting to do it. Aren't you going to thank Brad for the invitation?"

My father's voice came from the end of the table. "Yes, I believe a thanks is in order for such a kind invitation. Not many sophomore girls get to attend the Senior Sweetheart Dance."

So they'd all joined ranks against me. Suddenly I was really angry at the whole bunch, and instead of my sweet, *kind* self thanking Brad, I raised myself very straight in my chair and gave each one a fiery, defiant look. Then, before my courage failed me, I turned iceberg eyes on Brad and said coldly, "Thank you very much, Brad."

With what few scraps of dignity I could muster, I got up from the table and turned my back on them all, expecting every instant to be called back to the table. We are *never* allowed to leave without being excused, but nobody said a word, so I walked haughtily up the stairs—and then I cried.

Chapter
7

I cried so much the top of my pillow case dampened, then grew cold to my face. I turned the pillow over. That side was really icy, but at least it was dry. I thought about the horror of going to the dance with Brad—and he doesn't even *dance*! How mean can a person be?

Okay, Brad, I'm going to get something on you and fix you good. Like making myself stay awake and find out where you go when you slip down the stairs at night. It will serve the family right. They trust you so much and are sticking up for you instead of me.

Suddenly I sat up, my devious brain working away. And, Brad, old boy, I'm going to find out what you've got in that precious box and I'm going to tell everybody—*everybody*!

And then I shall say, "That's because you are such a loud-mouthed oaf and you told—" Wait a minute. I never told Brad a word about Brent. I've never mentioned his name to him. How does he know? Has he been watching me or something? Good grief! Surely I'm not as silly acting as Karen, that baby, idolizing Brad. I shuddered at the thought. No, of course I'm not. But maybe I ought to be a little more careful in the future. I don't want Brent to think—that is, I don't—well. Hmmm. I'll ask Laurie.

Gleeful at my thoughts of revenge on Brad, I started thinking about my new dress. Aunt Bessie designs a lot of dresses around here, and she is really good at it. Maybe a shocking pink chiffon . . . no! Black satin, strapless, with big rhinestone buttons down the front. I saw it in a magazine, and I knew Aunt Bessie could copy anything. And then I rolled on the bed and really laughed, knowing that I would have to spend a lot of time at Aunt Bessie's to get the pattern decided on, the fabric cut, measured, fitted, and all . . . and Brent would be there.

Brad, you may have done me a big favor, whatever your intentions were. If Brent gets to know me, who knows? Maybe he will ask me to dance, particularly when he sees me in that black satin with the rhinestones. I put on my pajamas and snuggled down in bed. I was still awake when my mother came in to kiss me good night, but I didn't open my eyes. I was already catapulting into tomorrow, consulting at my designer's about the black satin dress.

And I did. The day being unseasonably warm and bright, the snow melted to a dirty, wet slush as I walked to my aunt's after school. I'd worn my rain boots, but when I arrived, my feet felt as if they had been in ice water. I kicked the boots off at the door and warmed my feet with my Aunt Bessie's little electric panel in her sewing room.

Brent was nowhere in sight, but I kept drinking glasses of water in the kitchen, hoping he would come in, until Aunt Bessie insisted I bring my glass in the sewing room so we could get started.

She was not enthusiastic about the black satin. For one thing, she didn't have any and it would take weeks to get it on a special order. She opened her big trunk, which is a treasure chest of fabrics, and we started looking: French cottons, gauzy and soft to the touch, but too summery; silks, magenta and orange and bright green. I loved them, but Aunt Bessie thought they would be too slinky. I liked them even more after that, but she was firm. Then velvets, elegant and rich. And the deep colors, dark wine and forest green, looked mysterious, as if the pale winter sun falling on them through the window were golden candlelight falling on royal robes. I fell for the velvet. I held the forest-green length up to myself and studied my reflection in the long mirror.

Aunt Bessie pursed her lips and nodded. Then she narrowed her eyes the way she does when she's imagining the finished product.

"Yes, with your classic beauty—" (Aunt Bessie always says that just to make me feel good because I'm not stunningly pretty like Laurie.)

Then she eased out of her chair and went to the closet, which is also stacked with fabrics. She scrabbled among the sheaths of plastic she keeps the cloth covered with. "Yes, with your classic beauty"—there she goes again, I thought—"I think I might have something even better." She turned around, holding a plastic wrapped bundle. "I've been saving this for something special, and I think this is the time for it." She held up the length of fabric and let it fall into the sunlight. Pale lavender taffeta rustled as it moved, and in the light, it was iridescent: The folds became deep violet, shimmering. I had never seen anything like it.

Aunt Bessie held it up to me, and then we both looked at it in the mirror.

"Ye-e-es," she mused, her eyes tiny slits. "With your dark hair and green eyes, I think this is it." Her brown eyes opened up again. "What do you think? Do you like it?"

"I love it."

Her round face broke into a big grin. Unlike my mother, who is slender, Aunt Bessie is plump. Like my mother, she is an excellent cook, and her cakes, pies, cobblers, and cookies are masterpieces. It's no surprise she loves to eat her own cooking. She's generous with it, though, and likes to share with the community. Every church supper and picnic has some gifts from Aunt Bessie, and the school festivals, too. I've heard more than one student say they wish they could board at Aunt Bessie's, as Brent does, because the food would be sumptuous. Brent. Where could he be? I peered out the window, searching for him. But Aunt Bessie misunderstood my vigil.

"Yes, it's getting late. You'd better start home." She bustled around, picking up the fabrics, and I helped replace them in the trunk. "When you come tomorrow, we'll decide on the pattern, and I'll make adjustments to it." She handed me my coat, still talking. "And the next day, we'll cut. I have to get moving because next week Carol Jenkins's fabric for her wedding gown will be here and I promised her I'd start on it."

At the door, she held my chin in her hand for an instant. "You'll be lovely in that dress, Rose."

I kissed her chubby cheek. "Thank you, Aunt Bessie."

Outside, the wind nipped, and I wrapped my scarf closer around my neck. I scanned the road for Brent, but I was the only figure in sight. Though it was early, the sun was almost on the horizon and shadows were forming in the slushy ditches. I could see our house, tiny in the distance, and I ran clumsily in my rain boots as far as I could; then I walked, but in my imagination, my feet were dancing, skimming lightly in my gorgeous strapless dress, the lavender skirt whirling, glimmering, and turning to violet when the lights dimmed and Brent asked me for another dance.

Chapter
8

_I_ was still angry with the family, and I let them know it by being overly polite. Brad, I ignored completely, and right after my chores were done, I went upstairs and studied in my room. It was colder up there, though since I'm over the kitchen, the heat rises, and I have an electric wall heater. I was _not_ going to sit at the kitchen table and work with Brad. Actually, I was making a _C_ in that Lit class, which would make Dad flip when my report card came out. Brad could have helped me write an essay for Miss Dallaway. But I would rather have made an _F_ in the class than have anything to do with him.

My teeth were chattering soon, and I slipped under the covers before I had written even three paragraphs. I was just going to close my eyes for a minute, but the whole house was quiet when I woke up. Well, almost quiet. Someone was coming up the stairs. I looked at my clock: It was midnight. Then I heard Brad's door close. I'd caught him now. I _knew_ he'd been somewhere. I got ready for bed and jumped between the warm covers, my heart warmed even more now that I was *sure* about Brad's sneaking out at night. Now, at the proper moment, I would reveal all—as soon as I found out what was in the box. I drifted off to sleep pondering . . . pictures of his family? Raggedy clothes? Confederate money? All of the above? I knew it was nothing that rattled, unless it was packed very tightly, because Sam and I had already tested that when we'd picked up the box.

A key. I opened my eyes and stared into the darkness. It had a padlock; therefore, somewhere there was a key. Maybe it was time for me to make another little secret foray into Brad's room. I smiled to myself, turned over, and went to sleep.

The next morning, heavy gray skies darkened everything as Laurie and I walked to school. Laurie always asked about Brad because she's curious.

When I asked her how Brad could have known that I was . . . *interested* in Brent, she didn't hesitate to tell me.

"Yes, anybody who observes you would know you have an enormous crush on Brent Wilkinson." I was annoyed with Laurie for saying that and annoyed with Brad for observing it. So we talked about Brent. Not that there was anything new to say, but I can always talk about Brent, anyway. I wasn't ready to tell anyone about the lavender dress yet, even Laurie. If I told her about the dress, I would have to tell her about the dance and my having to go with Brad, and I just could not say those words. I choked even on the thought. I'd just have to live with it a while longer before I could talk about it. I could talk about my *C* in Lit, though, so I told Laurie that.

"You? Making a *C*? I can't believe it."

"I guess I don't listen well. I can see Brent, kind of at an angle, and then I start daydreaming, and I just tune out Miss Dallaway's voice." I kicked at a puddle of melted snow. "Then I get the assignment gummed up, and I end up appearing dumber than I am."

Laurie sighed. "That *is* dumb, Rose." Then she giggled. "Maybe you can get Brent to help you with your homework."

I stopped and clowned, striking myself on the forehead. "That's it! The perfect solution."

Laurie began to whisper. "Don't look now, but Brent and Pogey are behind us."

I straightened up immediately. My new resolution was to be very cool around Brent and let him speak first and everything. But I slowed my steps just ever so subtly, and I don't think Laurie even noticed.

Laurie changed the subject by talking about their new refrigerator, which has a box on the front that pours out crushed ice anytime you hold a glass under it.

"Who wants ice? I want a new dishwasher. Our old one has been broken a year." I was keeping an eye out for Brent and Pogey to pass us.

"Well, it'll be great next summer," Laurie said, and at that moment Brent and Pogey were beside us.

"Oh, hello, Brent," I said, smiling.

"Hi," he said to both of us, and walked on. Pogey did, too, and as soon as they were beyond us and I could see the back of Brent's parka, Pogey turned around and gave me a big grin—no, it was a laugh, and he was laughing at me. I felt my ears turn red, and I stared at the muddy ground we were walking on. Nothing Laurie could say would make me raise my eyes. I felt as gray as the day looked—and it got worse.

In Lit class, we were discussing the draft of our essays, which were due the next day. That is, those of us who had *done* the draft; I was not among that number. Miss Dallaway asked politely if she might see me after the last class in the afternoon. I stared at the wood on my desk the rest of the period, I was so humiliated.

After school, I hung out at the end of the hall until I was sure all the upperclassmen had left Miss Dallaway's room. Then I slipped into the room and sat in the very last back seat. Miss Dallaway was working at her desk, her small, white head bent over some papers, and I don't think she heard me. I stared out the window at the ominous clouds. They had grown darker all day, but the temperature had stayed warm. That usually means a snowstorm is on the way, Dad says.

"Rose." Miss Dallaway's soft voice crossed the room. "Come up to the front. You're not being punished. I just want to talk with you."

I walked to the front and sat in the first row. Miss Dallaway left her desk and sat in the seat across from me.

"You are a good student, Rose. Your teachers recommended you for this class on the basis of it, and you started the year well."

I was studying my fingernails and did not look up when she paused. Tears were poised behind my eyes, and I was determined that they would not roll. The stillness in the room pressed down on me; I wished I could melt like snow and be gone, disappear into the atmosphere.

Miss Dallaway continued. "I know this class is not too difficult for you. Are you bored with it? Have you lost interest?"

"No, oh, no, I haven't," I said quickly. "It's not that. It's just . . . it's just . . ." and I got stuck. How could I tell that dear little birdlike lady that my interest in Brent Wilkinson had outstripped my interest in literature?

"I have a reason for asking for a draft, you see. It is to assure that the essay will be almost prepared, except for the polishing, the day before it is due." Her voice became even more gentle. "Your recent grades have been *C*'s because you have not been giving your writing your attention. If you don't have your paper ready tomorrow, I am afraid you will drop to the failing list."

I swallowed hard. Failing was unheard of in my family.

"I will have that essay tomorrow, Miss Dallaway. I promise I will." And my own voice dropped with my shame. "And I'm sorry. I've . . . I've loved this class," and then I ran from the room and down the hall and across the schoolyard. The wind was just beginning to rise, but it felt good to my stinging face and the tears. My backpack bounced on my shoulders as I ran as hard as I could. I just wanted to run and run and run—and maybe I could run away from myself.

Chapter
9

*A*fter stretching myself out physically as far as I could, the cold air surging powerfully in my lungs—and my brain air-conditioned by the icy wind—I felt better as I bolted through the door at home. Also, my spirits lifted when I thought about the new dress. Mother had some hot chocolate ready—and still-warm brownies. I was in such a hurry to get to Aunt Bessie's that I tossed my backpack on the hall table, swallowed the chocolate standing up, and stuffed two brownies into my jacket pocket.

I changed from my sweaty rain boots and put on my loafers with some clean socks. I can run faster in them, and they look nicer.

I ran for a while and then walked, a few snowflakes drifting softly, tickling my face. Then I remembered the brownies; I munched and dawdled, thinking that the day, so badly begun, might turn out well after all.

Aunt Bessie had hot tea and Russian tea cakes waiting for me, and there was Brent, drinking Pepsi and gobbling Aunt Bessie's dainty little cookies like a dino-saur. I just nodded to him; it was not because I was sticking to my resolution, but because I was speechless at sitting at the same kitchen table with him.

"You're late, Rose," Aunt Bessie said. "I was hoping we could start earlier."

"I . . . I . . ." I could tell Aunt Bessie I'd had to do something for Mother, but Brent knew very well I'd had to see Miss Dallaway after school. I looked at Brent out of the corner of my eye, and he was grinning, waiting to hear what I would say. "I had to talk to one of my teachers."

Aunt Bessie looked startled. "You? That sounds more like Sam. What's the trouble?"

I wasn't going to be humiliated and scolded by Aunt Bessie in front of Brent. I was going to be cool. I smiled very big and waved my hand airily. "A tiny thing, Aunt B., just a tiny thing. Minutiae."

Now Brent was grinning even bigger. I grinned back. He rose from the table and said, "Well, I have to get that essay rewritten for Miss Dallaway. I learned last semester—the hard way—that when she gives a due date, she means it. Good cookies, Miss C. Later, Rose."

Later! I gulped and tried to be casual. "Sure, later, Brent."

I caught Aunt Bessie looking at me oddly, so I wasn't sure just how natural I'd sounded. Well, I need practice, I thought to myself, and making this dress will give me the chance.

A problem arose over the pattern. Aunt Bessie was

dead set against a strapless and I was dead set for one. She kept showing me patterns of every kind of dress since the world began, but I held out for a strapless. It wasn't that she didn't have a pattern for one; she did: several different kinds and two of them I loved. No. She wasn't having it.

When I wanted to know why, she had sixteen different reasons. The fabric wouldn't do well in that style, it was winter and would be too cold, my shoulders were too slender—reason after reason. Then, finally she told me the real reason: She thought I was too young to wear a strapless—too sophisticated for me. I was stung by that and sulked, really irritated with her. And she, by this time, was thoroughly irritated with me. It was a good thing the phone rang at that point and broke the tension.

It was Mother and she said it was almost dark, snowing, and since Dad had gone to the Farm Board meeting in Ames, I should stay at my aunt's for the night—if my clothes looked all right, and then admonitions to throw them in the washer and dryer if they didn't and to be sure this and be sure that and finally I got off the phone—smiling.

Aunt Bessie and I agreed on a truce until after supper, and I went in the kitchen to help. She had already made a huge chicken pie. My mouth watered when she opened the oven and I saw the golden crust with chicken gravy bubbling through the slits in the top. I made a simple salad, the corn bread cooked in twenty minutes, and we all sat down at the kitchen table. I

could hardly eat for minding my manners, but Brent
didn't have that problem. It was incredible how much
of the chicken pie disappeared. The dessert was vanilla
ice cream over blackberry cobbler. I had helped pick the
blackberries myself last summer and I said so, but Brent
was too busy with his third helping to pay much attention. What really astonished me was that Aunt Bessie
ate almost as much as he did. No wonder she has to let
out the seams in her dresses!

Brent went back to his room after supper, and we
cleaned up the kitchen. Fortunately, Aunt Bessie has a
great dishwasher—mechanical!—and we were soon
back at the patterns again. And a clash of wills.

Aunt Bessie spoils me in a way that my mother
does not, but when she sets her head to something, she
has that stubborn Carthage streak. Alas, I have it, too.
I was set on a strapless and I was digging my heels in.
After thirty minutes, we were silently staring at each
other without giving an inch.

Finally, Aunt Bessie sighed and held up the pattern
with the cap sleeves and the sweetheart neckline . . .
again.

"Rose, this is really a lovely design. Think how
beautiful it will be in that iridescent violet taffeta. Don't
you *honestly* think it's pretty?"

"It really is pretty, Aunt Bessie—" Her face began
to crinkle into a smile before I finished my sentence.
"—and I think it would look just darling on Karen!"

Her face fell.

I turned my head and studied her sewing machine

as if I found it fascinating. I don't have to concentrate on being stubborn; it comes naturally to me. What I really was doing was listening to see if I could hear Brent moving around.

But it was Aunt Bessie who moved, scrabbling in her shoe boxes of things she ferrets away. I watched her then, from the corner of my eye. She had something in her hand.

Lace. The most delicate, elegant lace I had ever seen, and it was wide, six inches or more. I couldn't resist turning and giving it a full look, it was so lovely. I didn't speak, though. I hadn't given in yet, and I wanted to know what she was up to.

"What about this?" she began. "This lace . . . this is Chantilly lace, a very fine piece." She suddenly gave me a blazing look. "I am *not* going to make you a strapless dress *this year!*"

I returned her blazing look.

"However . . ." She calmed down a bit and warmed to her new idea. "I will make one that comes just off your shoulder, just barely dropped, Rose—and with this piece of Chantilly lace all around the top."

She placed the lace on the lavender taffeta. It looked so perfect I was speechless—and a dropped shoulder was almost as good as a strapless. I think she knew she had broken our deadlock, because she rushed on with a final peace offering.

"And you can wear my amethyst earrings."

She gave me a quizzical half smile, shattering my reserve completely.

"Oh, Aunt Bessie, it's a great idea. Just great. And thanks. The earrings will be perfect."

She folded the lace away carefully. "And you will be the most beautiful girl at the dance," she said.

I laughed. I wouldn't be, of course, but Aunt Bessie was dear to encourage me. And it really was going to be a splendid dress.

Brent came out of his room as we were turning off the light in the sewing room.

"Get your essay finished, Rose?"

I stopped in my tracks and looked at him, horrified.

"I don't have my books. I left them at home!"

"Well, of course you did," soothed my aunt. "You didn't know you were going to stay here. I'm sure it will be all right." Then she looked at me. "Why, Rose, you're absolutely white. It can't be that serious."

"I'm afraid it is, Aunt Bessie. If I don't have that essay in the morning—" I hated to say it in front of Brent, but it had to be said: "—I'm going to be failing in Lit."

She gave me a puzzled stare. "That isn't like you, Rose," and she walked into her bedroom. I didn't say anything. She returned in a moment and held out her keys to Brent.

"Will you drive Rose home, please, Brent?"

You could have knocked me over with a feather. Nobody *ever* drives Aunt Bessie's car; she hardly even drives it herself. It is twenty years old and still smells new inside. We have a family joke that she would rather walk in the rain herself—which she does—than get her shiny black, old-fashioned car wet. She was really breaking her habits for me and I didn't say anything until I got my coat on. Then I kissed her on the cheek.

She came to the door with us, and in the yellow overhead light, the snow blew across the porch and turned gold. Already it mounded by the wood pile. Otherwise, the night was pitch black.

"Drive carefully, Brent. The roads will be slippery."

"I will, Miss C., I sure will."

I helped with the garage door, and I could hardly believe I was climbing into the old car with Brent Wilkinson. Wait till Laurie hears about this!

"Have you driven her car before, Brent?"

"Are you kidding? She walks everywhere herself—except to Ames. Good thing she does, too. She'd be a tub."

I was surprised but I laughed. It was a fact, all right.

Brent backed out slowly and carefully and then turned to the left when he got into the street. It was the wrong way to go to my house. I suddenly thought, He doesn't know where I live.

"Brent, we need to go the other way. I should have told you."

He laughed. "I know where you live, Rose, I just want to stop by Tillie's for a minute."

Tillie's! I sank back on the seat as if I'd been slapped. I couldn't think of a thing to say, but suddenly I wanted to go home very badly. I stared into the blackness ahead, watching the glitter of the snow as it passed through the beams of the headlights. Quickly, it became hard to see with the snow gathering on the windshield. Eerily, the wind whistled by the windows. An icy draft seemed to hit the back of my neck: Was it a fact or a feeling?

Brent left the motor on while he ran up to Tillie's door. In a moment I saw the door open. He went in. I looked away into the darkness ahead, and in a short time, Brent was opening the door, asking me to get in the back, and Tillie bounced into the front seat, chattering away. I was so numb I couldn't really translate what she was saying. It sounded like a foreign language. Finally, by concentrating, I got it. She wanted to go into town and see who was at the malt shop. And Brent said okay.

Brent had already started back toward Aunt Bessie's on the way to town.

I got my courage up then, and after a couple of stammering starts, I got my words out.

"I don't think we ought to do that, Brent. Aunt Bessie just loaned you the car to—"

Brent turned toward me in a fury. "You're right. She loaned *me* the car, and I'll be responsible for it. *You* don't have to worry about it." He turned back to the road. "Okay?"

"But—"

Tillie turned around and said, "Don't be such a wimp, Rose."

Suddenly furious myself, I started to say, "Tillie, mind your own business—" but the car skidded, and my heart skidded with it. We had stopped in front of Aunt Bessie's old farmhouse. Framed in the porch light with the falling snow, it looked like a Christmas card.

"Your mother thinks you're staying here tonight, Rose. She said you could. Just go in and stay." Brent's face was angry. I hesitated, and he spoke again. "Go on. It's okay. And it's not *your* business to tell your aunt anything. I'm a big boy and I'll tell her myself!"

I slowly opened the door and got out.

Tillie said, "Good night, wimp."

I slammed the door so hard the whole car shook.

I watched the tail lights, like two red eyes, as they shone on the road toward town, and then turned back to the house. Brent was right. He could talk to Aunt Bessie himself. I wasn't going to do it. I was going to walk home. In the distance, I saw the little yellow twinkles of the lights at our house. I shoved my hands in my pockets and started walking briskly, my loafers silent on the soft snow.

Chapter 10

S now crystals, forced by the wind, stung my face and collected on my eyelashes. I could hardly see. But then, there was hardly anything *to* see except the blur of whirling snowflakes—plus the tiny yellow lights of our house. I knew the way well, and even with everything blanketed with snow, I could place our twinkling lights between the distant lights of the Wards' house on the left and the Cranes' house on the right. Ours were in the middle and could guide me like a star. Besides, I'd walked this road all my life. When I was a little kid, I had even counted my steps: how many steps to the turn, then how many steps to the house. Maybe I should do that now, just to be sure, I thought. I figured I had taken about twenty steps already, so, keeping my eyes on the middle lights— twenty-one, twenty-two, twenty-three—I counted carefully, because the turn in the road was important. But my head was concerned about my feet; the snow was covering my loafers, then melting; my socks were drenched.

I made the turn okay, because the Wards' house lights moved farther away and my own came closer. I started counting again from one, two, three. . . .

My feet were so cold they were beginning to throb. Why in the world was I wearing my loafers? I remembered. I'd thought they'd look nicer—in case I ran into Brent at Aunt Bessie's. I ran into him all right, I thought bitterly, and he couldn't care less if I wore snowboots or went barefoot. I wonder where he was now. Aunt Bessie may seem like a gentle summer breeze, but she can turn into a genuine blizzard when riled. Like this wind, she has a cutting edge.

I snapped back from my drifting thoughts: I had lost my count. I strained my eyes to see the lights through the fuzzy blur of snow.

No lights.

Everything was pitch black.

I stopped stock-still, my heart thumping wildly.

I turned around and looked back at Aunt Bessie's to get my bearings. Could I have passed my own house? Impossible.

There were no lights behind me and none before me—none where the Wards' should have been and none at the Cranes'. Then I knew why: power failure.

I swallowed hard. Swallowing was hard, anyway, with my throat burning from so much cold air going in and out. Then I began walking as fast as I could.

No point in standing here and freezing, I thought.

Besides, all I have to do is walk straight ahead and I'll get home. I've done it a thousand times. I ought to have enough sense to know where my own house is, lights or no lights—but I *wish* I had kept my count.

One good thing, in a way, was that now my feet didn't feel cold or throb or anything at all. They just stumped along under me like stilts. I was beginning to feel nothing in my hands; the rest of me didn't feel too much cold, either. It worried me, but at least nothing hurt except my throat, which was raw. And I should be getting very close to home, if my sense of direction and timing had not completely gone haywire.

Yes. The feeling is right. I am home. I know it is right here someplace. The only trouble is, everything is dark. Maybe it's just a bit farther or maybe I've passed it.

Stupidly, I stood there, sure that I was in the road and afraid to leave it for fear I would start wandering in the fields. I could yell, but could I be heard above the howl of the wind?

I cupped my hands and yelled toward the left, where I knew our house was. Somewhere over there, anyway. I yelled until I was too hoarse and too tired.

I'm too tired to think, I'm going to sit down here in the road, and when Dad comes home from Ames in a couple of hours, he'll see me in the car lights. Besides, it will be warmer in a cocoon of snow. I sat down and squinched into my jacket like a turtle, hugging my knees and snuggling my face. It felt good to have my body all close together like that. It was almost like being warm.

It was lonely, though, lonely in all that darkness. Just me and the wind and the snow.

And I knew why I didn't feel the cold so much: I was beginning to freeze.

Chapter 11

*M*y mind spun with huge snowflakes, gorgeous snowflakes designed in lace, pale lavender, peach, and sky blue. Together they became a colored light—an angel, coming for me, an angel with glowing white robes and shimmering feathery wings.

Out of respect, I tried to stand, but I couldn't. It will be all right, though. An angel will understand.

Then she was singing, her beautiful clear voice ringing out so close I could hear it over the wind. But a strange song. But what do I know about angels? I guess they can sing anything they choose and it will sound heavenly. I just never would have imagined an angel singing "Hound Dog."

But the angel, lighted in splendor, was passing by me! Couldn't she see me?

"Hey, angel, I'm here! Angel! Angel!"

And the angel stopped, and her bright light shone in my face, and Brad's voice said, "My God, Rose!"

Then he slung me over his shoulder like a big sack

of potatoes. My body felt like a potato, but in my heart, at that moment, Brad was better than an angel.

I don't remember anything else until I saw the leaping of flames. I focused my eyes and saw Mother and Sam with a bowl of popcorn between them, sitting on the rug by the fire; their mouths were open in astonishment as they looked up. Then darkness closed in around me.

Faces swam, hazy and unclear, as if I were in deep water and could only see them through the murky subterranean depths: Mother, Dad, old Dr. Jinks, Brad, Brent—*Brent?* I knew I was under water because it was so hard to breathe; my throat burned and I coughed until my head ached as if I had been hit soundly with a hammer.

And then I returned to the land of the living.

And Brent *really* was sitting there in the overstuffed brown corduroy chair. His blond hair was slicked down as if he were going to church, and he was wearing a crisply ironed blue shirt (which matched his eyes). At first, I thought I was hallucinating, but I glanced around the room with the bright sunlight pouring in, and Mother, looking exhausted, was sitting on the stool at my dresser. When she saw that my eyes were open, she burst into tears. Then I was *really* shocked! I had never seen my mother cry.

Brushing her tears away quickly, she laughed and hugged me. Brent apologized over and over; I was not only speechless but embarrassed to death wondering how awful I appeared. I leaned up to see myself in the dresser mirror and was surprised to see that my hair was combed and I was wearing my mother's peach satin bed jacket with the soft ruffles at the throat. I looked almost glamorous—discounting the bloodless skin and dark circles under my eyes. I hoped that they made me look sad and mysterious rather than just plain sick.

I didn't have much to say to Brent except to tell him it was okay, and then the rest of the family—Karen, Billy, and Sam, and then Dad and Brad—all came in and there was a general hubbub with everybody catching me up on the news. But I was coughing and tired, so Mother shooed them all out. As I sank into sleep again, I realized she was holding my hand.

Chapter
_12_

_B_ rent and Laurie—not together—came to see me every day. And Dr. Jinks, almost every day, but I wasn't to go back to school for a week. The Sweetheart Dance was Saturday night. At least, I had gotten out of that! Brad had brought letters from school from my classmates and Laurie brought some, too. With all that attention, Dr. Jinks's cough medicine, and the beef broth my mother was pouring down me, I started feeling like my old self again.

The weather had tamed completely. The roads had been cleared, and I could see mounds of snow sparkling in the sun. I stood beside my electric heating panel and watched Brent as he walked to our house, something I thought could never happen. And, oddly, it was watching him that I liked the most. I wanted those moments to be slow motion: my standing with the backs of my legs all warm from the electric panel, the nice, soft quiet in my safe bedroom, and seeing Brent ambling in the snow. It was such a lovely scene with the leafless trees outlined in black against the sky and Brent's blue jacket sparkling in the sun-spears splashing through the branches. I wanted that scene and the delicious racing of my heart to go on and on, like a loved song you never tire of hearing.

Yet, when he arrived, and, of course, I had jumped into my bed and straightened the covers and was busily reading, I couldn't think of a thing I wanted to tell him. But, then, I didn't have anything to tell. Who would want to hear how much I had coughed or what pictures Karen had drawn or that Billy spent his evenings sitting on my feet? I asked him questions, though, to keep dead silence from falling. The trouble was that I kept asking the same dumb questions every day, sounding like a broken record.

How was Lit class?

Okay.

Had he seen my friend Laurie?

Yes, he'd seen her.

How were his other classes?

Okay.

How was the basketball team doing?

Lost—or won—and he would have been high-point man except that he had a swollen knee or a turned ankle or something.

What struck me as unusual was not what my mother did, but what she didn't do. Never, in all those afternoons, did she come smiling through the door with a tray loaded with chocolate-chip cookies or oatmeal-raisin, with steam rising from cups of hot chocolate or cinnamon-orange tea. I didn't have any appetite, but Brent could have handled my share with ease, and it would have given him something to do. And it would have given me a break from working so hard at conversation.

He did ask a question once; it startled me that he asked and what he asked surprised me even more.

"What does that Alabama kid have in the box?"

My mouth dropped open, and I hadn't the foggiest notion what to say. The only thing he ever asked me and I didn't want to admit that I didn't know!

Karen, bless her heart, saved me. Her curly head appeared shyly around the door. I greeted her with such enthusiasm that her big brown eyes opened a little wider, and she gave me a heavenly smile.

"I made you a picture."

While I was raving over the picture as if she were Andrew Wyeth—the picture, as far as I could tell, was a dinosaur—Brent mumbled his good-bye. He never asked me about Brad's box again. As usual, I was exhausted and coughing too much from talking or nerves or something.

Still, I wanted to etch in crystal and keep forever those moments every day when I stood dreamily at the window and watched him walking through the snow toward the house—toward me.

Now, when Laurie came, we chattered away as if we hadn't seen each other for years. And my mother treated us like duchesses. She used the rosebud teacups on Grandmother's silver tray and served all Laurie's favorites: strawberry preserve tarts or lemon squares and, one day, even sugared pecans. I teased Laurie that she didn't come to see me; she just came to eat. Mother joked and laughed with Laurie, and twice she sat down with us and had tea as if she had all the time in the world, and I knew she didn't. It was strange.

The first time Laurie came after I returned to the land of the living, her bronze curls sprang up like curly feathers when she pulled off her woolly cap. She was conspiratorial.

"I saw"—and she lowered her voice—"I saw Brad's box when I came down the hall. Have you found out anything?"

"Well, no, Laurie. After all, I've been here in bed, you know."

She gestured toward the door. "It's just down the hall. Couldn't you—"

"Laurie, are you crazy? You know my mother and dad. If I snooped around in Brad's room again—" I shook my head. "I'd be grounded so long a trip to the library would be the event of the year."

"Yeah, well, it just seems like such a waste to be so close and—"

I interrupted again. "Forget it. Now, what's the juicy news?"

And she had some.

One of the Teague twins had fallen in love with the bandmaster. And Brent was out of favor because he didn't bring me home that night in Aunt Bessie's car. In fact, he barely got the car to town and back in the storm.

A furious Aunt Bessie had told him he couldn't board at her house anymore, and because his family lives too far from school, he now had to board with the Cranes, who have seven kids.

"And Mrs. Crane isn't nearly as good a cook as your aunt is." Laurie paused for breath. "Did you know Brent has come to your house every day, Rose? Even when you were running a high fever and didn't know anybody?"

I began smiling smugly and then stopped.

"Good Lord, I hope Mother didn't let him in here!"

"No, she didn't—I know because she wouldn't let me in, either. But what do you think? Would you ever have dreamed it?"

Now I really did smile. "Never, Laurie, never."

"What do you talk about when he's here?"

"Uh . . . oh, you know, this and that. Just stuff."

Laurie sighed. "Just asking. I'll probably never have to worry about carrying on a conversation with an admirer! I'll just follow under the light of your star."

"Aw, Laurie, cut it out."

"I'm serious," Laurie said. "Everybody is concerned about 'beautiful little Rose.' "

I smirked at that.

"Come on, Laurie. I've been sick but I haven't grown stupid. Just because I got lost in the snow I've become beautiful? Even if I had, which I haven't noticed, nobody has seen me in ten days!"

Laurie looked at me, her blue eyes round and serious.

"Rose, I'm telling you the truth. I heard them myself."

I angled my head and gave her my nonbelieving smile.

"It's like this, see, Rose," which is the way she talks when she's about to impart some great theory of hers. "See, everybody probably always thought that, but they weren't talking about you before. See what I mean."

"You don't have to make me feel good, Laurie. I already feel good."

"Rose! I *heard* it, I tell you." She counted them off on her fingers as she talked. "The principal was talking to your English teacher and he said, 'Beautiful little Rose,' and Meridal Larson was talking to Pogey and she said, 'Have you heard how beautiful little Rose is?' and that freshman kid, that guy with all the freckles? Like mine," she grimaced. "Well, somebody was telling him what happened and he didn't call you little—actually, you're a foot taller than he is—but he sighed and said, 'She's so beautiful.' You've got a secret admirer in that kid, Rose."

I stared at her. Could this be true, or was Laurie's imagination running away with her? I stood up on the bed and looked in the mirror, crossing my eyes and baring my teeth; Laurie doubled over in her chair, giggling.

Then she told me everybody was impressed with Brad and thought he was wonderful because he had rescued me from a frozen death in the snowstorm.

Suddenly, Laurie leaned over close to the bed and

whispered, "What was he doing out walking in the snowstorm, anyway, Rose?"

Yes, what *was* he doing out walking in the snowstorm? I was so grateful that he *was* that I hadn't really thought about *why*.

"I don't know, Laurie. I really don't," and I laughed. "But, believe me, I'm glad!"

"He's filling out with your mother's good cooking, and he's a good-looking guy. Some of the seniors—girls—are calling him a hunk."

I crowed over that. "Brad? A hunk?" I rolled on the bed, laughing at the thought. Laurie got up to leave, and as she stood in the door, she said, *"I* think he's a hunk, too."

Brent came over after Laurie left, and he asked me to go to the Sweetheart Dance. I could hardly believe my ears. At the back of my head, I was aware that he knew I couldn't go, but I enjoyed the moment, anyway. Nobody outside the family knew I had planned—*been forced*—to accept Brad's invitation, and I didn't say a word about it.

I thanked Brent, and after he left, I sat up in bed, smiling, thinking what a wonderful time we would have had. My lavender dress would be flashing amethyst and violet, and we would be laughing and talking about everything and having such fun together. Suddenly the strained afternoons with Brent and my struggling to make conversation came back to me. I frowned, remembering. So far, we hadn't done much laughing and talking together. We hadn't had much fun.

Of course not. We hadn't had a chance, that's all. I erased those thoughts and went back to the rosy feeling of Brent's having asked me to the dance. I focused on that moment, then started thinking about supper. I was hungry for a change.

I was hoping to go downstairs to eat, but Brad brought in a tray with my soup, toast, orange juice, and cherry cobbler. He said Mother was very tired and that Dad had sent her to bed and served dinner himself. Mother had already cooked the cobbler and the soup, and I was glad: I've eaten my dad's cooking before. Brad said that Dad would be up to see me after a while and that I could come downstairs to eat the next day.

It was the first time Brad and I had been alone to have a real conversation since we'd met on the road in the snow. I had, of course, thanked him, but we hadn't talked about it.

He sat in the overstuffed chair while I ate. Suddenly he started laughing. Puzzled, I looked at him. He said, "Did you know you were croaking, 'Angel! Angel!' in the road that night?"

I began to laugh, too.

He said, "Here I was walking along with my flashlight when what do I see in the middle of the road, almost right in front of the house, but this lump of snow, hoarse as an old bullfrog, saying, 'Angel! Angel!' I thought I was losing my marbles."

"I had already lost mine. Your flashlight looked like a shining angel to me and I thought she was singing. I know angels sing, but she was singing 'Hound Dog.' " I waited a moment and then I said, "What were you doing out there in a snowstorm when you could have been eating popcorn by the fire?"

Brad's face suddenly changed and his grin faded. He actually opened his mouth twice, but nothing came out.

Then Dad came through the door, a white apron tied around his waist and drying his hands on the dish towel he had slung over his shoulder. Brad seemed overjoyed to see him and immediately got up and sat on the dresser stool. Dad took the chair, after kissing me on the cheek. He told Brad he could begin bringing my assignments home the next day. Dr. Jinks had forbidden it until now.

Brad took my tray downstairs. I was nervous about what Dad was going to say. I know that the dumbest thing a person can do is set off walking in the snow at night without a light. And my parents didn't allow it even *with* a light—not me, anyway. If I started talking first, maybe I could beat him to the draw.

"I'm really sorry, Dad. I know it was a stupid thing to do, but Brent just dumped me out. . . ."

Dad held up his hand to stop me.

"Brent didn't just dump you out, Rose. He let you out in front of your aunt's house, and there was no reason for him to believe you wouldn't go in."

I dropped my eyes to the patchwork quilt on my bed; he was right, of course.

"You couldn't have chosen a more dangerous thing to do, but I'm not going to harp on it. You have suffered a lot for your poor judgment. Brent *could* stand a few lessons in being more responsible, but what you did was your own fault. Of course, I didn't like his behavior at all, and neither did your mother—and certainly not your aunt."

He stood up. "Rose, I never would have found you that night. The highway patrol advised us to stay off the highway until the snowplow could clear it. I spent the night in Ames."

I pulled the threads of my coverlet and then looked up at him.

"What was Brad doing out in that snowstorm?"

He studied my face for a moment, and then he said, "Why don't you ask him, Rose?"

Chapter
13

I did ask him the very next chance I got. He brought my assignments from my teachers and said he would help me. We were in the living room by the fire. I was all curled up in a blanket, loving being downstairs and out of the bedroom. Brad settled in a big chair close to the fire and said, "Where would you like to start?"

I said, "What were you doing out in the snowstorm?" And getting even more bold, I said, "And where do you go every night?"

His eyes widened a little, and then he stared into the orange and red flames. Finally, without looking at me, he said, "That's private territory, Rose. However, *if* and *when* I consider you a real friend, I'll tell you." Then he turned those big brown eyes on me, the flames casting a strange red gleam on them. I stared back with a combination of surprise and rage.

Of all the rude remarks! After I had taken him into

my house and treated him like part of the family. Well, my *family* had taken him in, anyway, and I'd had to sacrifice a new dishwasher. At least, *maybe* we would have gotten a dishwasher if we hadn't gotten Brad.

What farm families *don't* have in our area is lots of cash money, except after harvest. We have plenty of rich black soil, and plenty of work to do, plenty to eat, and old, heavy, well-insulated and heated houses—but money, no. After harvest, which in our case is corn, we have money, but it has to be stretched out to be used for the whole year—for shoes, clothes, repairs for machinery, seed corn, animal food, emergency illness—and each person in the family is a drain on it. That's why I equal the expense of Brad to the expense of a dishwasher. Even *I* could figure out that we couldn't have both.

There was plenty I could have said to him—ungrateful, arrogant, selfish, *secretive.*

But I decided not to lower myself by saying anything at all.

I rose to my most haughty height and prepared to make a royal exit, my nose in the air. I tripped over the blanket and fell headfirst on the rug. Brad didn't move, didn't laugh, but let me scramble up, red-faced. Without looking my way, he said again, "Where would you like to start?" and he opened our Lit book.

Feeling like a fool, I crawled back into the blanket and whispered, "Let's talk about that essay I have to write before Monday."

That's when I learned what a slave driver Brad could be. I had some notes, but he made me write a complete rough draft; then we read it, cut some lines, added some lines, and read it again. I was tired, but I was still furious about his crack ". . . if and when I consider you to be a friend . . ."; I wasn't going to give him the satisfaction of seeing me give up. I hung in there and wrote the essay again. My head was beginning to ache and I was coughing, but I stayed on. I would have written it five more times before I admitted I was tired and weak. He read it after the second draft and said, "Okay, let's quit."

"That one's good, huh?" I was going to make him say it.

"No, I just meant let's quit for tonight. You can do another draft tomorrow."

Ugh!

This time, when I started to make my haughty exit, I first picked up the blanket from around my feet and queened it up the stairs without a word to Brad.

I did write another draft of the essay the next night, but Brad had gone to the dance. I guess I was glad I couldn't go, but I had gotten kind of used to the idea of going; it was lonely after I came downstairs and found he was gone. He hadn't said another word about the dance to me. He said he couldn't dance; why did he go? He could have had the grace to stay home because I couldn't go. But I didn't care what he did. I *did* wonder who Brent was dancing with.

I didn't feel too great, my throat still scratched, and I went upstairs early, about as blue as I could get. When I passed Brad's room, I stuck out my tongue at his box and then I stopped. Somewhere there was a key. Why try to find out what's in the box some other way when the simplest solution was the key?

Now where does he keep that key? I wondered. He doesn't wear it around his neck or I would see the chain.

I backtracked to the door of his room and scanned it. Bed carefully made, gleaming mahogany dresser with mirror and matching huge mahogany armoire—my grandmother's, old but beautiful—no closet, small rug by the bed, rack on the wall with his Sunday blue tie and his battered work hat.

Mother won't let anyone come upstairs to disturb me if she thinks I've gone to bed, I said to myself. And I can hear the burble of the ancient black-and-white TV downstairs. Perhaps . . . perhaps there's no time like the present.

It didn't take me long to go through the dresser drawers—not much in them: sweater, socks (I pinched the toes to see if anything was hidden there), underwear, T-shirts, and some letters from his family, held together by a rubber band. I just looked at the return address. I wouldn't invade his privacy by reading his letters.

The armoire, used as a closet, had a jacket, dress shirts, and bedroom slippers. I looked in the pockets of the jacket and in the toes of the slippers. I ran my hand, stretching up, along the top of the armoire. No key.

I checked between the mattress and the box springs, then straightened the bed. At that point, I decided he must be carrying it with him, but why? The dust on the top of the box proved that he didn't open it.

In frustration, I grabbed the blue tie and shook it. Then I grabbed the work hat and hit it against the wall. Bouncing out of the hatband and flying across the room came the key.

It landed with a little click on the floor in the doorway.

It landed close to some brown-stockinged feet also in the doorway.

I looked up from brown socks to brown eyes.

Brad leaned on the doorframe, watching me; his muddy loafers were in his hand, a newspaper for cleaning them under his arm.

The blood that surged to my face was so hot it could have raised blisters. Momentarily, I was paralyzed, still holding the hat in my hand.

Brad seemed to have turned to stone; I couldn't even hear him breathing. I reached down and picked up the key and was going to put it back in the hatband when he spoke.

"Just hand it to me, Rose. I don't think I'll keep it there anymore."

I couldn't look in his eyes. I placed the key in his outstretched hand, edged past him, and, head down, almost ran to my room.

"Good night, Rose," he said as I closed my door.
How could I ever face him again?
Good grief, suppose he told my parents!
I did a lot of tossing and turning before I fell sleep.

Chapter
_14_

S unday breakfast is not a big deal at our house because everybody is getting ready for Sunday school and church; I was allowed to stay home that next morning and Brad stayed, too. The family had never insisted that he attend church, but he often did with the rest of us. I knew he hadn't told my parents about my invasion of his room because neither of them said anything about it; and they would have. You could bet they would say plenty. I had to be grateful for that.

Still, I would rather have coughed all through church than face Brad. I stacked the dishes in the sink and started washing like crazy, my eyes on the soap suds. Ordinarily, I am only too happy when someone picks up a dish towel and starts drying, but when Brad did it, I was so nervous I dropped Karen's favorite Snoopy glass, the one Aunt Bessie gave her for Christmas; I stood looking at the shards on the floor, my limp hands dripping soapy water on the green linoleum.

Tears started running down my face. I was trembling.

"Karen's favorite glass. That's just great."

"Don't worry, Rose. We'll get Karen another one."

And suddenly, I started babbling, a faucet I couldn't turn off. "Oh, Brad, I'm sorry about the key. I'm sorry. You're really so good and innocent and sweet and kind, even, and I don't know why I'm such a bad person! I'm sorry. . . ." And then I sobbed so hard I couldn't speak.

Brad pulled me toward him and put his arms around me and hugged me to his chest. And he just held me there, my wet face dampening his starched shirt. He held me close without saying a word, until the sobs subsided and I was just sniffling.

Then he let me go and, stepping over the glass, got a clean dishcloth from the drawer and gently dried my face. He steered me toward the living room.

I pulled back and jabbered, "I've got to clean up the glass. I've got to finish the dishes. I—I've got to put the ham in the oven. I—"

He held my arm firmly and kept pushing me toward the fireplace. "No, Rose. That will wait." He sat me down in the big chair and pulled the wool throw over my knees.

I started to cry again, feeling like such a fool. I rarely cry, and here I was, practically floating away in tears. I didn't understand it. Maybe it was my punishment for being a sneaky, bad person. I hid my face in my hands. I heard Brad crumpling newspaper, and then the fire beginning to crackle, catching the dry kindling.

Brad pulled my hands away from my face and held them both in his own. He was sitting on the floor by my chair. I couldn't stop the tears. They just kept coming.

"I—I don't know why I'm crying like this—"

"Rose." He squeezed my hands tightly between his own. "Rose. Take a really long, deep breath. That's it. Now another one."

I started to speak but he said, "No, don't talk. Another deep breath. Go on, another and another."

I did what he said, and the tears stopped. I felt like a drenched rag, but the feeling of bubbling and roiling had gone. I was myself—a sad self—sitting by a warm fire with Brad still holding both my hands.

"Don't worry about the crying. You've been very, very sick. You're fragile right now. You're as fragile as the glass you dropped. It will pass when you get strong again."

He released my hands and got up. "Now I'm going to put the ham in the oven. What temperature?"

"Three twenty-five, but—"

"You close your eyes and breathe like I showed you."

I did, and soon he was back, holding my hands.

"You said I was innocent and sweet, Rose, and I'm not. I'm not innocent and sweet, and only sometimes am I kind. You don't know me, Rose. You fantasize. You imagine what a person is like and then you believe your fantasy to be real. I've observed you doing it."

Brad not innocent and sweet? But he was right. I didn't know him. And though he had started talking about himself, he had ended up talking about Brent. I stared into the leaping flames. I wanted to worship Prince Brent's royal blue eyes from afar; I didn't want those royal blue eyes looking at me at close range where I had to struggle to make some kind of conversation. What I knew about basketball was limited to the style of the cheerleaders' outfits. What I wanted was my dream of Brent; I didn't want to cope with the real live boy.

I said, "Brent," but Brad didn't comment.

What he did say was, "You're not a bad person, and I don't want to hear you ever say that again. Don't even dare think it. And as for what happened with the key last night, it's okay. Let's forget it. All right?" He grinned at me. "All right?"

"All right." And with Brad grinning at me like that, I felt it really *was* all right.

He got my Lit book from the end table and handed it to me. "We're way into *A Tale of Two Cities* in Miss Dallaway's class. Start reading while I take care of things in the kitchen. Were we supposed to cook anything besides the ham?"

How do you like that; "Were *we* supposed to . . ."

"No, Mother has everything else ready, and Billy and Karen have to set the table."

"Okay, read on. We'll talk about it this afternoon. I want to read your essay, too," he said, as I watched him walk away into the kitchen to do my chores. I don't care what he says. I think he's sweet and kind.

Even with such a fine Sunday lunch, I couldn't eat much. Mother had made my favorite dessert—a luscious snowcapped chocolate pie—and I ate a sliver of it just to please her, but I was afraid I was going to be sick. I must have been turning pale green because Mom suddenly told me to go into the living room, that she would take care of the kitchen.

I fell asleep in the chair by the fire and didn't wake up until Karen and Brad were sitting on the rug, talking in whispers. I watched them through veiled eyes; Karen was telling Brad she had a headache and would he please give her a head rub. Brad grinned, rubbed her head about five times, and her long eyelashes fluttered down. She curled up like a cat at his feet, fast asleep. I watched him leave and come back with her shabby security quilt and wrap her up in it, tucking in the sides.

Don't tell me you're not sweet.

When Brad saw that my eyes were open, he said softly, "I read your essay, Rose, and it is really good. That last draft did it."

Billy came in then with a defiant look at me. "Mom and Dad are going for a drive, and she said I could watch TV if I turned off the sound while you studied." He kicked the rug and ruffled the edge. "Won't you and Brad *please* study in the kitchen, *please?*"

"Maybe Rose ought to stay by the fire," said Brad.

I said, "Turn the sound real low, and, just this once, you can get close enough to ruin your eyeballs. How's that?"

He did his Superman act to the TV and stuck his
nose two inches from it.

I hadn't read a half page of *A Tale of Two Cities*
before there was a knock on the door.

Brent! Brent was coming over this afternoon, and
I had completely forgotten about it. I struggled to get
the throw off my knees, and Brad said, "Do you want
me to get it?"

"*No!* I mean, no, I'll do it."

I opened the door and there he stood, royal blue
eyes and all. Without giving it a second thought, I heard
myself saying, "Brent, I really have to study this afternoon. I've got to catch up, you know. I go back to class
tomorrow."

His eyes opened wide with surprise, and a hurt
look crossed his face.

Good Lord, I was rude and abrupt.

"But come on in. You can study with us. We're
working on *A Tale of Two Cities.*" I held the door open
wider, and he looked into the living room: Karen asleep
on the floor, Billy with his nose on the almost-silent TV,
and Brad lying on his stomach in front of the fireplace,
his Lit book open.

Brad said, "Hi, Brent. Come on in."

Brent studied the scene a few moments and then
said, "Some other time, Rose," and walked away.

I stood looking after him with a feeling of loss. I
knew he would not come back again, and it was not

— **89** —

only Brent-the-boy walking away; it was also Brent-the-dream, lost forever.

I shivered, closed the door, and returned to my reading without a word. Billy was now drowsy, and he curled up beside Karen; Brad pulled the quilt over them both. The only sound was the soft flickering of the fire. When my eyes began to water from fatigue, Brad took the book out of my hands.

"Just close your eyes and listen," and he began to read to me.

He had the most beautiful reading voice, even with his funny accent. It wasn't so funny anymore, or I'd just become accustomed to it. I never knew *A Tale of Two Cities* was so interesting. Or maybe I never heard it before, because I was always trying to watch Brent out of the corner of my eye, or fantasizing driving up to the malt shop with him or something.

Brad made the characters come alive. When he got to the great sacrifice of Sydney Carton—where he gives his life for his friend—and he says, "It is a far, far better thing that I do, than I have ever done," I felt the tears coming again. I could not believe I would be in tears over English literature. Or maybe it was because I wanted to learn to be a real friend—the kind of friend Brad had been to me this morning when he'd quieted me in his arms.

I went to sleep that night remembering how my wet face felt against his warm shirt. And looking forward to more evenings reading in front of the fire.

Chapter
15

*N*o more evenings by the fireplace: Spring was beginning to burst upon us and that is hard-work-time on our farm, as on all the surrounding ones. Dad and Brad, if not working at our place, were helping the neighbors. They worked in the barn under the lights with the machinery, unloading seed sacks arriving by truck and parceling out shares of the huge bags of special fertilizer bought together with several neighbors. Sometimes they didn't have dinner with us but shared a meal where they were working, as the neighbors sometimes did with us. I was kept busy helping Mother on those nights, and the rest of the time, I was making up the work I had missed. I now had a $B+$ in Lit class and my other grades were all A's.

Briefly, we would have snow flurries, but it all melted rapidly on the warming earth. The daffodils, crocuses, and tulips were showing their leaves, sometimes through a little patch of snow. Courageous little things they were, because sometimes the wind was still bitter when Laurie and I walked to school. Laurie accepted philosophically, but with some wonder, my loss of Brent-the-boy and Brent-the-dream. She said she missed my clowning about it. I didn't tell her about the key and the box and Brad, but she sensed something. "You've changed, Rose," she said. "You're more beautiful and you're more sad." I laughed at that, but when she asked if I had found out anything more about the box, I said I hadn't given it another thought, that it was a dull subject. She looked surprised and didn't ask me again.

And Brad. I hardly ever saw him, even though he lived down the hall from me. He was getting up at five to study; then, as soon as it was light, he was helping Dad. In Lit class, he grinned at me when I made comments—as I never had when I was in my fantasy world—and once I must have been particularly brilliant because he silently applauded when I finished talking.

For a while, I loitered after school, thinking we might walk home together, but I never saw him leave. Later, I learned from Sam that Brad was excused from study hall early and was already home working.

I had my work, too. As soon as the peonies began to bud and the daffodils were in full yellow bloom, Mother started planting all the annuals—cosmos, zinnias, gladioli, and feeding the scores of old-fashioned roses for summer bloom. Our peonies are fifty years old; they were my grandmother's, and some of the roses are cuttings from bushes older than that. There are over a hundred rose bushes on our property, and that takes a lot of feeding. My mother knows the name of every one, and when we tramp over the yard in our rubber boots, I always feel she is talking to them like old friends. Whatever it is, it works. In the summer they are unmatched splendor.

Then there was the vegetable garden to plant and take care of. This garden was just for family food: eating, freezing, and canning for the winter. The men readied the rich black earth, but Mother and Sam and I planted and took care of it—weeding and, later in the year, watering if we didn't get enough rain. Work, work, work. We were all so tired at night that we fell into bed and, at least for me, dreamless sleep.

The last hot, sticky June day of school, Brad came home with a grin that glowed like neon. He had made the honor roll: all *A*'s last quarter. He and Dad had a private conference. Brad would go to summer school. I didn't hear what the details were, but Brad apparently wanted to make up what he had missed so he could graduate.

My final report card so pleased Mother and Dad that we had a Sunday-night celebration. Sam, of course, while not in actual disgrace, had grades that were nothing to celebrate. Karen and Billy were always the fastest in their classes. I thought at first that the festivities were only for me, but because Brad was at the top of his class, too, we shared the honors.

We had supper on the picnic table in the yard among the roses: fried chicken, potato salad, baked beans, and a big chocolate cake with chocolate frosting.

It was a wonderful evening with the scent of roses hanging over us, fireflies flitting as dusk fell, and the family in as relaxed a mood as I could remember in a long time. I told Dad he looked as if he had lost ten pounds—since I'd seen him one day last winter—and hadn't seen him since. He laughed and said I looked a lot better than I had when I'd tried to turn into a snowball. But Mother said, "He has seen you, too, all of you. He always goes in and checks on each of you before he goes to bed, no matter how late it is."

And that suddenly made me think of his checking on Brad. But he knew where Brad went at night. Did Brad still go out? I had been so tired all spring, I was asleep by the time I hit the bed, and I had never heard him again. Maybe *he* was too tired to go out.

And then Dad made a kind of announcement. He said, "Brad will have finished all his high-school work after summer school and is going to go to the university this fall."

"The university!" I said, astonished.

Brad tried to turn his sternest look on me, when he said, "What's so strange about that? I'm old enough, you know," but he couldn't stop smiling; I had the feeling he might take off and soar right over the buckeye trees any moment.

I suddenly felt a great emptiness. I wanted to know him so much better. I wanted to spend time with him. I wanted to dry my tears on his shirt front. I wanted him to hold my hands.

I watched him now talking to Dad. He had

changed so much from the scrawny, tall boy we had gawked at that first snowy night. He was tan from the morning sun, with farm chores before school, and the afternoon sun, with the plow and the hoe after school. Those thin shoulders had become muscular with the pitch of the hayfork. My father had said he was worth three hired hands any day.

The university! I felt young—too young—and scraggly; I wondered what the college girls would think of Brad.

Now that I knew I wanted to be with him, I became so shy I couldn't go near him at all. Anyway, that summer I rarely had a chance. He was up working in the field before I stirred, then gone to summer school, working again, and studying like a fiend alone in his room at night—with the door closed. Even Sam was not allowed to make his nightly visit.

Summer was already a drag. Laurie had gone to her grandmother's, and the Crane kids had never really been friends of mine. The vegetable garden was growing on its own. I finished most of my housework early, read library books, and strained my eyes looking for Brad in the cornfield.

If time moved slowly for me, it stumbled to a boring halt for Billy and Karen, who were accustomed to being surrounded by their school friends.

One blazing afternoon, Mother found the two of them, with Dad's saw, cutting clumsily on the bottom of Brad's box. Mother made Karen polish all the silver in the house. Because my ancestors have lived here forever and handed down everything, Karen was busy for a whole week. It was a big, hard job for a little girl. Billy had to hoe around all the roses—and over a hundred roses is a lot of hoeing. And also, Mother, who usually walked with them down to our swimming hole two or three times a week in the hot weather, restricted swimming.

Wow! Poor kids.

I felt sorry for them and guilty, too, because nobody knew—except Brad—about my episode with the key. I was amazed at the kids' courage with the saw, and I quizzed them privately about the box, but they hadn't discovered anything.

Through the window, I watched Billy, leaning on his hoe beside the lavender roses. It set me thinking. Brad had said about himself that he wasn't sweet and innocent; could he have something in the box he was ashamed of? But then why would he have brought it with him? No. I sighed. Guess again.

Chapter
16

*T*he whole house smelled of peaches, the rich, ripe juicy fragrance of summer. Jars lined the kitchen shelves, the peaches making rosy amber mounds behind the sparkling glass.

My hands and arms were stinging from the peach fuzz, mixed with my perspiration, in this muggy kitchen, but I was too hot to care.

Mother must have been dead on her feet, scouring that big kettle, and all that steam was making it harder to breathe.

I picked up the basket of peach peelings for the pigs and then saw Mother's face, scarlet from the heat, her hair damply curling around it. She raised one hand to brush sweat from her glistening cheeks. She'd started working at five this morning, but she'd let me sleep in.

"Mother, why don't you take a nap? On the screen porch, where it's cooler."

"The floor."

"The floor?" I ran my foot across the linoleum—

sticky and gummy from melted sugar, peach juice, and golden bits of peach flesh.

I started toward the door with the basket for the pigs.

"I'll clean the floor," I said. As Mother opened her mouth to speak, I went on quickly, reading her mind, "I'll scrub it and wax it and it will be perfect. I promise it won't be my usual sloppy job. I promise."

She laughed, stepped closer to me, and kissed me lightly on the cheek. Then she pulled her apron tie with one hand, and the soggy, stained apron fell away from her damp dress. She tossed the apron into the washing machine at the end of the long kitchen. And looking back over her shoulder, she smiled at me.

"Thank you, Rose." And she headed for the screened porch.

I slipped my clogs on my bare feet, because walking on the gravel path would have been like stepping on hot coals. Then the merciless sun hit my head. Everything looked whiter, somehow faded: the bright orange of the gladioli, the purple of the verbena, and the blue of the lobelia. Even the grass was bleached less green. Maybe I was just imagining it because I was so bored. I dumped the peach peelings into the trough. Two of my favorite pigs, Nemo and Dido, lolled in the mud, coating themselves with damp grayness, but they didn't even greet me with a grunt.

Back in the kitchen, I filled the mop bucket with warm water, squeezed in several drops of detergent,

and dipped the mop in. Then I really got into it. I
sloshed the frothing, bubbly warm water all over the
kitchen floor an inch deep, squishing and sliding in my
bare feet, swirling the mop in every corner and splashing a double deluge in front of the stove, where I had
peeled the peaches.

I heard the screen door open and I turned. Brad,
flat on his back, skidded, slid, careened the full length
of the long kitchen. He sailed by me as if he were on
ice.

When he stopped by the washing machine, he
placed one elbow on the floor, raised his head, and
said, "Hi."

I started laughing then. I laughed until I was
blinded by tears. Brad was standing when I managed to
see again.

"I came to get you to go swimming, but I see
you've got your own water slide here." He skidded a
few more steps in the soapy slush, laughing.

I leaned on the mop with a sigh.

"Would I love to go swimming? Yes. But it'll take
me an hour to get all this soap up and rinse it and—"

"Hey, did I say I wouldn't help? Give me a mop.
I'll show you how it's done."

I handed him the other mop from the broom
closet, and he started swishing up the soap and wring-
ing the mop over the bucket. "Where are the kids? They
can go, too. We'll be through here before you know it."

"It has to be perfect. I promised."

"Of course, what other way is there?" and even as

— 99 —

he talked he was working a mile a minute. I was impressed.

I explained, hustling to keep up with his pace, that Karen, Billy, and Sam had gone with Dad to the Hardware Fair.

"Mother's resting. She's been canning peaches all day—as you can see."

Brad looked up at the rows of jars. He wrung the mop while he talked.

"They look beautiful like that, but they are even more beautiful in those cobblers she makes."

With the two of us sloshing away at the floor, the soapy water disappeared and the rinse began. I know I blushed when we backed into each other a few times, but it was a lot less boring working with Brad. In fact, it wasn't boring at all.

When we'd finished with the clear-water rinse, the floor gleamed wetly, but dry spots began to appear by the time the mops were hung outside.

"Okay, let's go," Brad said, grabbing my hand in his big, warm paw. I didn't want him to drop my hand, but I couldn't leave yet. Oh, don't let him leave without me, I thought.

"I still have to let it dry and then wax it," I said. And then I added sadly, because decency—sometimes a rare thing with me—demanded it, "You go on for your swim. You never get an afternoon off."

He gave me a long look, his deep brown eyes gleaming in the quiet kitchen. He was still holding my hand, my now-very-sweaty hand.

"But I wasn't ready to *leave.* I just meant I should get our picnic ready while you finish up. Then we'll go. Okay?"

I grabbed an old towel from the ragbag and, on my hands and knees, dried the places where the water still glistened. I heard Brad rattling around on the back porch where the fruit was kept, opening the big refrigerator and taking out ice cubes. I was glad he was getting the food; I was too excited to think what to take. A picnic with Brad. I didn't believe it. I just couldn't believe it.

I waxed the far end away from the door first; when I turned, Brad was leaning on the doorframe, watching me so closely that I blushed, stammering, "You—you can't—you can't walk on this after I've waxed the rest. Do you have everything?"

"Miss Rose," he said, in an exaggerated Alabama drawl and with a crooked, slightly wicked smile, "I have everything!"

At last I finished and we stood outside, holding open the door to survey the floor. It shone like dark green glass.

"Perfection, as promised," Brad said, clutching the big brown paper sack in his arms.

"Oh, my swimsuit!" I stopped so suddenly the rocks from the gravel skittered.

"Swimsuit? For the swimming hole?" Brad pushed me forward. "Your cutoffs are the proper thing. Besides, if we walk home in our wet clothes, we'll stay cooler longer." He tapped my arm. "That's physics, kid."

The swimming hole was closer to the road than it was to the house. We trudged across the cornfield, then down a long row of corn, the sun beating on our heads. I was quiet, thinking that if I'd had a wish to come true today, I couldn't have improved on this. We would have a chance to talk, to know each other. I watched Brad's long, golden-tan legs walking ahead of me on the path.

"I'll break trail," he had said, "and do combat with any brontosaurus or pterodactyl. You handle the snakes and wolves."

Finally, as the path dipped, I saw the great oaks sheltering the pool. A stillness surrounded the hot afternoon as if the world had stopped. Even the usually noisy bluejays and blackbirds were quiet. We stepped into the shade. The temperature seemed to drop the moment my head was out of the baking sun.

Patchy green spots of light patterned the pool, then deep cool green reflected the canopy of leaves. Brad set the sack down and, with a running leap, clowning, grabbed his nose, drew up his knees, and shattered the glassy surface of the water.

He came up immediately, his sun-bleached hair plastered to his skull, grinning, and then backstroked toward the other side.

I sat on the grassy bank, dangling my feet, enjoying the caress of the water after the hot walk, swishing and splashing back and forth.

Brad had disappeared. The surface of the water was undisturbed except for my swinging feet.

He shot up like a porpoise right in front of me, laughing at my surprise.

"No lazing about, Miss Rose!" He grabbed my ankles. "Exercise!" he shouted, sliding me over the grass right into the pond. I came up gurgling, shot a stream of water into his face with the palm of my hand, and raced away in a crawl as he gave chase; white water foaming, our arms flailing, feet churning, we raced toward the far end; I was choking from laughing with my mouth open.

Brad caught one of my feet, and I twisted to get away. I turned completely in the water, slapped my arms on the surface, spray flew high, glittering in the sun—and through the glittering spray I saw bright splotches of red on the bank.

Red?

Against the backdrop of the shadowy dark green oaks.

Red?

The game had stopped as I focused on the bright color. Brad looked, too.

Red, all right. A red bikini. And red dangling earrings, huge, and a red beach towel dropped on the grass. And white blonde hair. Too white. Josette Bingham. Senior. In Brad's class.

I couldn't imagine what Josette was doing here. On second thought, oh, yes, I could.

Neither Brad nor I had spoken in our surprise, but the water was out of my eyes and I saw her clearly. The red suit barely covered her bosom, and the skimpy sides—sides!—were only a red string. Her tan was perfect, and her slender thighs glistened with suntan oil.

"Hi, you two." She smiled and swung her head, the long red earrings dangling wildly about her throat. "I dropped by to see you, Rose, and your mother said you were probably down here."

"Hi." My greeting was not enthusiastic, but then I was astonished. Josette had never dropped by to see me in my entire life. In fact, she'd rarely spoken to me.

"Come on in, Josette," Brad said. "The water's fine."

"The rest of my gang—Sharon and Tillie—are in the car. I'll just yell for them." She walked through the trees slowly, while Brad and I watched her hips, covered a fraction by the strip of red, sway from side to side.

My heart dropped all the way to the bottom of the pond and was lying there with the old shoes, hiding trout, and mud-covered rocks. I could hardly speak.

"Did you know they were coming, Brad?" Unintentionally, it came out a choked whisper. Brad turned innocent eyes to me.

"No, but it's okay. We have enough food for an army, so don't worry."

I lowered my eyes and saw only the murky green water. He doesn't understand at all, I thought. No, maybe I don't understand.

"I think I'll get out for a while, I think," I said

stupidly. I swam to the side and scrambled up, rolling over on the grass just as the three girls sashayed—no other word for it—through the oaks. The splotches of red were Josette, sunshine yellow on Sharon, and a one-piece white suit on Tillie. One piece, all right, but sides open to the waist and the front gathered like a diaper. The top was open to her navel. I looked down at my frayed cutoffs and my faded blue T-shirt.

I thought this was going to be the worst afternoon of my life.

They didn't swim. They lounged on the bank and conversed with each other and occasionally shouted to Brad. He swam and I lay on the bank—the bank away from the girls—with my arm over my eyes. I felt terrible. Then water splashed on me. Brad took the hand I had across my face.

"Are you rested now, Rose?" he said softly. "Why don't you come back in for a swim before we eat?"

I opened my eyes and he winked, then pulled me headfirst in the water. But we didn't play any more games. I swam and dog-paddled and floated and he did, too, with occasional shouts from the loungers on the bank. Then we laid out the fruit and the lemonade—they shared a cup—and they chattered to Brad about college and people in the senior class. You would have thought I hadn't been born yet, but then I wasn't trying to make stunning conversation with them, either; you might say I was just barely polite.

After that, we packed up the sack, they sashayed through the trees, and we hurried home. Brad had to help with the animals. I took the sack from him and he jogged toward the barn. I kicked the rocks on the gravel path, loitering, sulking in the late afternoon sun. Brad gets one afternoon off the whole summer and what happens? Three contenders for the Miss America title rain on my parade.

Chapter
17

Not only were there no more swimming-hole days for Brad—the men were all involved with the harvest—but there were no more lolling, lazy days for me.

All those seeds we had planted in the cold, wet spring had sprung, blossomed, and now weighted their stems with beans, peas, squash, and bell peppers. And tomatoes! Huge beefsteak reds, pear-shaped yellows, and bright red cherry tomatoes, the size of walnuts. And the work: picking, peeling, slicing, chopping. Mother never seemed to be out of the kitchen, and I felt that I lived there. Mostly, it was canning and freezing for the winter, but the tomatoes were made into sauces—spaghetti sauce, chili, soup base—I sickened on the smells of oregano and thyme hanging in the humid room.

None of this vegetable harvest came as a surprise. I had been through it before, but I did have another kind of surprise: Girls who had graduated with Brad dropped by to see me. However, because Brad was nowhere in sight and we were working in the hot kitchen, they never stayed longer than ten minutes. I began to be grateful that he was unavailable in a very real way. Still, however, I held out hope for the last summer festival of the season. The Harvest Picnic in Old Peach Tree Park loomed heady and dizzy for me. I was afraid the men would not take the day off, but Dad said it was his one-day vacation in summer and that we were all going to help him celebrate. He was already peering into the mammoth basket that looked far too small for the mountain of food Mom was trying to fit into it.

When we got close to Old Peach Tree Park, the air was fragrant with the last ripe peaches and with the scent of the huge, pink cabbage roses blooming in profusion all through the grounds of the park. From that distance, the picnic crowd, shifting and mingling, kaleidoscoped on the trampled grass under the trees. Even the edge of the placid lake seemed to froth with multicolored fish, which, we could see as we drew nearer, really were varisized children, shrieking and splashing. The "older" bunch had a volleyball game going. They immediately yelled for Brad to join them. I couldn't hang around, so I wandered off with two of the freshman girls, leaving Karen with some of her friends.

I stared at a puffy black cloud, always there on the picnic scene, knowing it was a hailstorm for sure.

From behind me, Brad said, "Let's go for a swim."

All at once, that heavy rose-and-peach-perfumed

air I had drawn into my lungs seemed too much for me; I thought I would burst. Then the first hailstone hit me. Brad grabbed my hand and we ran. I was so glad everybody else was dashing for the pavilion or they might have noticed I wasn't running; *I was flying.* I simply soared through the hailstones with Brad.

As soon as all the grandmothers, grandfathers, babies, dogs, and all other moving creatures were under the roof of the dance pavilion, the hail stopped. The band had collected itself, anyway, and the music started.

We leaned on the rail, and finally Brad said, "I'd ask you to dance, but I don't know how."

"I don't know how, either, Brad, but I'll bet if we practice at home we can learn and pretty soon we'll be able to outdance anybody!" How great that's going to be, I thought.

"I can't," Brad said slowly. "I just can't. I've got to work and study every minute—*every* minute."

I'm not good at hiding my emotions. You could have seen my face fall for a country mile.

"Listen, Rose," he said, "it's like this. I've got an opportunity—a real opportunity, and I've got to grab it by the collar like—"

I laughed, somehow encouraged by the low excitement in his voice.

"Like Pogey Holland?"

Brad grinned.

"Yes, just like Pogey Holland."

We picnicked with the rest of the family, then finished stuffing ourselves with homemade strawberry ice cream that the Wards had brought and shared with us. Watching Brad talking with the men, I knew he was going to grab opportunity by the collar, but I wished we could learn to dance. We helped pack up the picnic gear, and then, as darkness began to fall, a bright light over the trees signaled the moonrise.

"Rose, let's walk home."

Walk home? I'd love it.

"I'll have to ask Dad."

"I'll ask him. Come on."

Trying to maneuver into the car, Dad had Karen over his shoulder. In her characteristic way, she went to sleep when she was tired wherever she was. She looked like a rosy angel—when asleep!—with her long eyelashes brushing her cheeks. Mother and Billy were already in the car. Sam was still talking to some of his cronies.

"Mr. Carthage, Rose and I would rather walk home. Is that okay with you?"

Dad studied us both for a moment. "All right. Sam is walking with his friends, too. Will you stay behind them? I don't want Sam making detours."

"We'll do that," Brad said.

Dad caught Sam's eye and motioned with his head toward home. The boys started in that direction, punching each other and laughing. Brad and I ambled slowly behind them.

The moon, an enormous pearl, already shed enough light to make black shadows behind the boys. I looked up at the stars in the navy blue sky; they were as white as glittering Christmas lights. Brad held my hand in his and we strolled without speaking. It was all so perfect that I was suspicious; surely any minute, some gorgeous, sophisticated girl would drive up in a sleek yellow convertible to give us—us? *Brad!*—a ride; or Josette would—

"Rose."

Brad's voice startled me.

"I want to explain about my going out at night, why I was out in the snowstorm when I found you."

I opened my mouth, then closed it. For once, I said to myself, be quiet and listen.

"I went out at night to sing."

Did he say *sing?*

And he continued, "Do you remember I told you I was not innocent and sweet?"

"Yes, but I didn't believe you."

"I always sang, see, and I got into this rock group with some other guys. We got stars in our eyes and decided to be rich and famous, to be professionals. My mother said no—my father is dead—but I sold everything I owned, which wasn't much except a good collection of recordings."

The moon went behind a cloud, and so I could hardly see Brad when he said, "I bought myself a sequined suit—coat, vest, pants—the works!"

I stopped in the street. Brad in a silver sequined suit? Brad as lead singer in a rock group? Sweet, innocent Brad?

He saw my face, and I'm sure he could read it.

— 111 —

"It's true, Rose. We dropped out of school, took off in a car one of the boys owned, and were going to make the big time on the East Coast."

"You mean—like New York?"

"New York. Chicago. Atlantic City."

"Your group must have been *good!*"

Brad laughed, not too cheerfully.

"We were good enough to play for high-school dances in small towns in Alabama, but we weren't good enough to do more than that."

Suddenly it hit me. Brad's sequined suit was in the box!

"And what did you do with your gorgeous sequined suit?"

"That gorgeous sequined suit was full of sweat from being worn every night, spotted with mustard from hot dogs eaten in haste between shows, the sequins flopped off in spots when I sat down, and one night, one of the guys got sick on it. It definitely was not gorgeous anymore, Rose. When I got home, I burned it in a rusty barrel in the backyard, along with a lot of fantasies about being a big rock star."

"But what happened in New York?"

"New York! We never even made it out of Alabama. Except for the guy with the car, we hardly had enough money to eat. We stayed in cheap rat holes. We were exhausted from hours of driving, all of us crowded into the car like sardines, plus the instruments. Then playing a gig in some dirty honky-tonk. It wasn't glamorous or exciting or glittering. It was horrible."

"So you gave up and went back home?"

Brad hesitated. We walked in silence for a few minutes before he answered, his voice low. "I wish we had. Oh, I wish we had."

He stared straight ahead when he told me.

"One of the guys—the one with the car—had money. He started using drugs—hard drugs. One night, when we'd finished a gig in a crummy little town and were spending the night in a fleabag motel, he overdosed."

Now that he had started talking, he raced on.

"He died, Rose. Right in the room next to mine, he died. You see why I say I'm not innocent and sweet?"

"But you weren't on drugs, Brad."

"We all used 'uppers' to help us get up in the morning or to stay awake after driving all night—and 'downers' to try to sleep when we got the chance. I never want to live like that again."

I almost whispered. "Do my folks know about all this?"

"Yes, they knew it before I came, and I talked with them afterward."

We turned into the driveway and stopped in the front of the house. Night-blooming jasmine scented the moonlit yard.

"A lead singer. Maybe when you're older—"

"No, Rose. I do not want that life. If I sing, it will be because I love it. I will sing in ways that are fun to me."

He held both my hands and stood facing me.

"My singing at night after I got here helped me. I was so used to spending hours practicing and listening to music—to being with the group who were my friends. And one of them was dead Singing, with me, was almost an addiction, and yet it helped me break the loneliness of a new life, a new home—to leave the grief behind me and start new—a bridge."

Brad's whole story had a physical effect on me: I think I was in shock because I began trembling and stood looking at Brad as if I'd never really seen him before. He faced me, expressionless, giving me time to let the story sink in.

The front door opened, throwing a beam of yellow light across the yard. Mother and Dad stepped out on the porch. Dad reached back and switched off the light, and together, they looked at the moon.

Sam! Good Lord, I'd forgotten I ever had a little brother.

I whispered to Brad, "Sam. Where is he? Did he get home?"

"Yes. I watched him all the way. He went into the house ten minutes ago."

He led me toward my parents on the porch.

"Beautiful night, isn't it?"

Mother answered, "Yes, it is."

He opened the door and said to me, "And a beautiful day, Rose."

Chapter
18

And then Brad was gone. He took the bus to visit his family in Alabama, and Dad had to hire two hands to help with our farm and to co-op with neighboring farms. The harvest was in full swing when school opened again, and I was swamped helping Mother and keeping up with my lessons.

The leaves on the buckeye trees were barely edged with gold when Brad returned, only for the day, and then had to leave for the University of Iowa.

Sam had saved up and gave him a sterling silver pen. Mother presented him with her brown suitcase, old as the hills, but carefully washed with saddle soap and showing its patina of fine leather.

Brad didn't take the box.

"I'll just leave it here in the room, if it's not in your way," he said, as we clustered around the door, fighting over the chance to carry some of his gear to the station wagon. We were packed in the car as Dad drove to the station, but we would have hung on the back bumper rather than miss seeing him to the train.

Mother cried. Dad shook hands with him and said he'd never known anyone to work as hard. Brad kissed Karen on the cheek; he hugged Billy and even *Sam,* who never allows *anyone* to hug him.

I was standing back, utterly miserable; life was going to be so dull, so barren with just tomatoes and pigs and dull boys like Brent for the rest of my life. Nothing exciting was ever going to happen to me again, with Brad gone. Even mopping the kitchen and talking about Lit was fun with Brad. Tears were banked behind my eyes; I was afraid to blink, or they would roll unchecked forever and ever.

Brad came to me and put his hand on my shoulder. Passengers were boarding the train, and the train itself was wheezing, growling, warning everybody noisily.

Brad leaned close to speak over the din.

"Send me some letters, will you? I may be very lonely."

I certainly hope so, I thought, desperate and selfish.

Then, as the train gave a huge *whoosh,* Dad called, "Brad!"

Brad leaned close to me and shoved something into my hand, then just brushed my cheek with his lips; he closed my fingers over the thing in my hand and said, as he turned to run, "Guard that for me."

He dashed toward the door of the train and jumped on, waving to the rest of the family.

I didn't look up or move because I had blinked and the tears had begun to roll; through that blur, I was staring at the key in my hand.

And every time I walked down the hall to my room, I thought about that key, but I didn't stop. Well, *once,* I stood with the key, staring at the box. Then I remembered Brad's brown eyes, watching me the night I'd found the key in the hatband. I left without opening the box and after that, I secreted the key away in the back of my Bible.

For six weeks, Brad wrote us postcards—all of us—with pictures of the university: the chapel, the football field, the ivy-covered administration building. The postcards all read alike: "Hi, how are you? I am fine and getting adjusted. Will write soon."

I was bitterly disappointed and wrote postcards of the same kind to him.

I didn't mind at all that Brent never asked me out again. But some of the junior boys did. I went to the class Halloween party with Jimmy Franklin, but I wasn't interested, and I'm sure Jimmy knew it, even though I was polite. Laurie *was* interested in Jimmy, and I was glad when she bubbled to me that she was going to the movies with him. We were still good friends, but I didn't discuss Brad with her and she sensed that our confidences had a barrier. It wasn't that Brad had asked me not to tell his story of the rock group; he hadn't. It was that I felt it was his story and I'd decided to let him tell it himself.

At last a real letter came, but the envelope was addressed to Mom and Dad—a family affair.

We were at the dinner table when Dad opened it and read it aloud. I could hardly sit still—Dad was so *slow.*

> Dear Folks,
>   Wonderful news! I have a job for the *Farm Co-op* newspaper, writing a weekly column about the students from our town—and it is fun! (Pays, too.) I have to get around and meet people and find out what's happening. Maybe journalism would be a good major for me—but plenty of time to decide that. I'm taking English, math, history, and journalism.
>   And the box, yes, the box. You can tell my friends, Karen, Billy, Sam, and Rose, that they can have the box. I don't need it anymore. I entrusted the key to Rose—

Sam exploded. "*You* have the key! Well, what's in the box?"

Karen yelled, "Yeah, what's in it, Rose?"

"I don't know," I said. "He trusted me. I didn't open it."

"You didn't even *tell* me you had the key," Billy sulked.

Sam got up and stretched out his hand. "Women,"

he muttered, and then, "Well, hand it over. He said we could. Come on."

"Don't you want to hear the rest of the letter?" Dad asked.

I was already out of my chair. Sam headed for the stairs, calling back, "We'll hear it after we open the box."

Karen and Billy were pushing each other to see who could follow Sam the fastest, and they—I should say *we*—raced up the stairs. I got the key and Sam unlocked it.

There was nothing in the box.

Sam and Billy and I just looked at each other. Karen burst into tears.

"He took everything out," she wailed. "I thought he would leave *something* for *me!*"

"Naw, he didn't," said Billy. "Nothing's been moved since the day we sawed on it. I've checked real careful. See, it's just the way it was."

"What a phony guy!" said Sam bitterly. "There never was anything in it. He's just fake, that's all."

I was surprised, but listening to them, I began to understand.

We trailed slowly down the stairs where Dad was still waiting at the table, the letter lying in front of him.

Sam was the first to speak.

"There wasn't *anything* in the box. An *empty* box! Brad's a—a—an *imposter,* that's what he is."

"Oh?" said Dad, "what did he tell you was in the box, Sam?"

"He never did *say* anything was in it, but there was *something* in it that's not there now," I said.

"What? What?" cried Karen.

"You won't understand, Karen, but his pride was in it."

Dad said, "Let me finish the letter, please."

He read:

> The box was important to me because—well, somehow, I couldn't face it just bringing myself—*I* didn't seem like enough and *I didn't have anything else.* I don't need the box anymore—thanks to all of you. You helped me through a bad phase in my life, and I am very grateful.
>
> I have investigated student loans and if my grades are up after this semester—and they will be!—I will be eligible.
>
> You are all invited to the Family Weekend on the first of next month. Please come. I want to show you all around this exciting place.
>
> Love,
Brad

Oh, I thought, he didn't mention *me*—exciting place, *I'll bet!*

"There's a note addressed to you, Rose." Dad held out a little white scrap of paper. The kids were so thunderstruck that they didn't even shout, "What's in it?"

I took the note up to my room. I could hear Karen

yelling then, and my mother's firm voice saying something about "Rose's privacy."

Dear Rose,
     The Journalism Club is having a picnic for members on the Family Weekend (while the parents attend a lecture)! Will you go with me?
                                        Miss you,
                                        Brad

P.S. I sing in the college chorus. I'm learning some folk songs, light classical, and we'll sing the Christmas carols for the university.

P.P.S. An essay I wrote for my English class has been accepted for the college magazine, freshman section. Guess what it's about? The night I arrived at your house with my box. I'll send it to you when it's published—you're in it, of course.

P.P.P.S. I haven't learned to dance yet, have you? Remember the night I went to the Sweetheart Dance? I only went to work an hour's shift behind the soda-pop bar.
     Oh, Rose, I miss you more than you can ever know.
                                        Brad

     I smiled at the first stars outside my window. No, Brad didn't need his box anymore.
     I called down the stairs.

"Does anybody want Brad's old phony empty box?"

"No," came the shout. "What good is that old thing?"

"I'll take it then," I said. I dropped Brad's letter into it, closed it, and turned the key.